The *River* of adventure

Enid Blyton, who died in 1968, is one of the most successful children's authors of all time. She wrote over seven hundred books, which have been translated into more than forty languages and have sold more than 400 million copies around the world. Enid Blyton's stories of magic, adventure and friendship continue to enchant children the world over. Enid Blyton's beloved works include The Famous Five, Malory Towers, The Faraway Tree and the Adventure series.

Titles in the Adventure series:

The *River* of adventure

Enid Blyton

MACMILLAN CHILDREN'S BOOKS

First published 1955 by Macmillan Children's Books

This edition published 2007 by Macmillan Children's Books
a division of Macmillan Publishers Limited
20 New Wharf Road, London N1 9RR
Basingstoke and Oxford
Associated companies throughout the world
www.panmacmillan.com

ISBN 978-0-330-44838-3

5 7 9 8 6 4

A CIP catalogue record for this book is available from
the British Library.

Typeset by Intype Libra Ltd
Printed and bound in the UK by CPI Mackays, Chatham ME5 8TD

Contents

1

Four miserable invalids

'Poor Polly!' said a small sad voice outside the bedroom door. 'Poor Polly! Blow your nose, poor Polly!'

There was the sound of loud sniffs, and after that came a hacking cough. Then there was a silence, as if the person outside the door was listening to see if there was any answer.

Jack sat up in bed and looked across at Philip in the opposite bed.

'Philip – do you feel you can bear to let Kiki come in? She sounds so miserable.'

Philip nodded. 'All right. So long as she doesn't screech or make too much noise. My head's better, thank goodness!'

Jack got out of bed and went rather unsteadily to the door. He and Philip, and the two girls as well, had had influenza quite badly, and were still feeling rather weak. Philip had had it worst, and hadn't been able to bear Kiki the parrot in the bedroom. She imitated their coughs and sneezes and sniffs, and poor Philip, much as he loved birds and animals, felt as if he could throw slippers and books and anything handy at the puzzled parrot.

Kiki came sidling in at the door, her crest well down. 'Poor thing,' said Jack, and she flew up to his shoulder at once. 'You've never been kept out before, have you? Well, nobody likes your kind of noises when their head is splitting, Kiki, old thing. You nearly drove Philip mad when you gave your imitation of an aeroplane in trouble!'

'Don't!' said Philip, shuddering to think of it. 'I feel as if I'll never laugh at Kiki's noises again.' He coughed and felt for his handkerchief under the pillow.

Kiki coughed too, but very discreetly. Jack smiled. 'It's no good, Kiki,' he said. 'You haven't got the flu, so it's no use pretending you have.'

'Flue, flue, sweep the flue,' said Kiki at once, and gave a small cackle of laughter.

'No, we're not quite ready yet to laugh at your idiotic remarks, Kiki,' said Jack, getting back into bed. 'Can't you produce a nice bedside manner – quiet voice, and sympathetic nods and all that?'

'Poor Polly,' said Kiki, and nestled as close to Jack's neck as she could. She gave a tremendous sigh.

'Don't – not down my neck, please,' said Jack. 'You *are* feeling sorry for yourself, Kiki! Cheer up. We're all better today and our temperatures are down. We'll soon be up and about, and I bet Aunt Allie will be glad. Four wretched invalids must have kept her hands full.'

The door opened cautiously, and Aunt Allie looked in. 'Ah – you're both awake,' she said. 'How do you feel? Would you like some more lime juice?'

'No, thanks,' said Jack. 'I tell you what I suddenly – quite suddenly – feel like, Aunt Allie – and that's a boiled egg with bread-and-butter! It came over me all at once that that was what I wanted more than anything else in the world!'

Aunt Allie laughed. 'Oh – you *are* better then. Do *you* want an egg too, Philip?'

'No, thanks,' said Philip. 'Nothing for me.'

'Poor boy, poor boy,' said Kiki, raising her head to look at Philip. She gave a small cackle.

'Shut up,' said Philip. 'I'm not ready to be laughed at yet, Kiki. You'll be turned out of the room again if you talk too much.'

'Silence, Kiki!' said Jack and gave the parrot a small tap on the beak. She sank down into his neck at once. She didn't mind being silent, if only she were allowed to stay with her beloved Jack.

'How are the two girls?' asked Jack.

'Oh, *much* better,' said Aunt Allie. 'Better than you two are. They are playing a game of cards together. They wanted to know if they could come into your room this evening and talk.'

'I'd like that,' said Jack. 'But Philip wouldn't, would you, Phil?'

'I'll see,' said Philip grumpily. 'I still feel awfully bad-tempered. Sorry.'

'It's all right, Philip,' said his mother. 'You're on the mend – you'll feel yourself tomorrow!'

She was right. By the evening of the next day Philip was very lively, and Kiki was allowed to chatter and sing as much as she liked. She was even allowed to make her noise of an express train racing through a tunnel, which brought Mrs Cunningham up the stairs at once.

'Oh *no*!' she said. 'Not *that* noise in the house, please, Kiki! I can't bear it!'

Dinah looked at her mother, and reached out her hand to her. 'Mother, you've had an awful time looking after the four of us. I'm glad you didn't get the flu too. You look very pale. You don't think you're going to have it, do you?'

'No, of course not,' said her mother. 'I'm only just a bit tired racing up and down the stairs for the four of you. But you'll soon be up and about – and off to school!'

Four groans sounded at once – and then a fifth as Kiki joined in delightedly, adding the biggest groan of the lot.

'School!' said Jack, in disgust. 'Why did you remind us of that, Aunt Allie? Anyway I hate going back after the term's begun – everyone has settled down and knows what's what, and you feel almost like a new boy.'

'You *are* sorry for yourselves!' said Mrs Cunningham, with a laugh. 'Well, go on with your game – but do NOT let Kiki imitate aeroplanes, trains, cars or lawn-mowers.'

'Right,' said Jack, and addressed himself sternly to Kiki. 'Hear that, old thing? Behave yourself – if you can.'

'Mother does look a bit off-colour, doesn't she?' said Philip, dealing out the cards. 'I hope Bill will take her for a holiday when he comes back from wherever he is.'

'Where *is* he? And hasn't anyone heard from him lately?' asked Dinah, picking up her cards.

'Well, you know what old Bill is – always on some secret hush-hush job for the Government,' said Philip. 'I think Mother *always* knows where he is, but nobody else does. He'll pop up out of the blue sooner or later.'

Bill was Mrs Cunningham's husband. He had married her not so very long ago, when she was the widowed Mrs Mannering, and had taken on Dinah and Philip, her own children, and the other two, Jack and Lucy-Ann, who had always looked on her as an aunt. They had no parents of their own. All of them were very fond of the clever, determined Bill, whose job so often took him into danger of all kinds.

'I hope Bill will come back before we return to school,' said Jack. 'We haven't seen him for ages. Let's see – it's almost October now – and he went off into the blue at the beginning of September.'

'Disguised!' said Lucy-Ann, remembering. 'Disguised as an old man, do you remember? I couldn't think who the old, bent fellow was who was sitting with Aunt Allie that night he left. Even his hair was different.'

'He had a wig,' said Jack. 'Buck up, Dinah – it's your turn. Have you got the king or have you not?'

Dinah played her card, and then turned to the radio nearby. 'Let's have the radio on, shall we?' she said. 'I feel as if I'd like to hear it tonight. Philip, can you bear it?'

'Yes,' said Philip. 'Don't pity me any more. I'm as right as rain now. Gosh – when I think how miserable I was I really feel ashamed. I wouldn't have been surprised if I'd burst into tears at any time!'

'You did once,' said Jack, unfeelingly. 'I saw you. You looked most peculiar.'

'Shut up,' said Philip, in a fierce voice. 'And don't tell fibs. Dinah, that set's not tuned properly. Here, let me do it – you're never any good at that sort of thing! Dinah – let *me* do it, I said. Blow you!'

'Aha! Our Philip is quite himself again!' said Jack, seeing one of the familiar brother-and-sister quarrels beginning to spring up once more. 'You've got it, now, Philip – it's bang on the station. Ah – it's a skit on a burglary with John Jordans in it. It should be funny. Let's listen.'

It *was* funny, and Aunt Allie, having a quiet rest downstairs, was pleased to hear sudden roars of laughter upstairs. Then she heard a loud and prolonged whistle and frowned. That tiresome parrot!

But it wasn't Kiki. It was John Jordans in the comical play. He was the policeman, and was blowing his police whistle – pheeeeeeee! Then someone yelled, 'Police! Police!' and the whistle blew again.

'Police, police!' yelled Kiki too, and produced a marvellous imitation of the whistle. 'PHEEEEEEEE! Police! Police! PHEEEEEEEEEEEE!'

'Shut up, Kiki! If you shout and whistle as loudly as that you'll have the *real* police here!' said Jack. 'Oh, my goodness! – I hope Kiki doesn't start doing this police-whistle business. She'll get us into no end of trouble! Kiki – if you shout "Police" *once* more, I'll put you down at the very bottom of the bed.'

Before Kiki could make any reply, a knock came on the bedroom door – a most imperious knock that made them all jump. A loud voice came through the door.

'Who wants the police? They're here. Open in the name of the law!'

The door opened slowly, and the startled children watched in amazement. What did this mean? Had the police really come?

A face came round the door, a smiling face, round and ruddy and twinkling, one that the children knew well and loved.

'BILL!' cried four voices, and the children leapt out of bed at once, and ran to the tall, sturdy man at the door. 'Oh, Bill – you've come back! We never heard you come home. Good old Bill!'

2

What a surprise!

Bill came right into the room and sat down on Jack's bed. Kiki gave a loud cackle of pleasure and flew to his shoulder, nipping the lobe of his ear gently. Aunt Allie came in too, smiling happily, looking quite different now that Bill had arrived.

'Well, what's this I hear about four miserable invalids?' said Bill, putting an arm round each of the two girls. 'You'll have to get up now I'm back, you know. Can't have you lazing in bed like this!'

'We're getting up tomorrow at teatime,' said Lucy-Ann. 'Bill, where have you been? Tell us!'

'Sorry, old thing. Can't say a word,' said Bill.

'Oh – *very* hush-hush then!' said Dinah, disappointed. 'Are you going to stay at home now?'

'As far as I know,' said Bill. 'I sincerely hope so. It looks to me as if somebody ought to look after your mother now. She's gone thin. WHY did you all have to have flu together, so that she couldn't have any of you to help her?'

'It was very selfish of us!' said Jack. 'And even you were away too, Bill. Never mind – everything seems all right when you're here – doesn't it, Aunt Allie?'

Mrs Cunningham nodded. 'Yes. Everything!' she said. 'Shall we all have a picnic meal up here in the bedroom, children, so that we can have a good old talk with Bill?'

It was a very hilarious meal, with Kiki more ridiculous than usual, blowing her police-whistle whenever she felt like it. Everyone got tired of this new trick very quickly, even Bill.

'Bill! Bill, pay the bill, silly-billy, silly-bill!' shouted Kiki. She got a sharp tap on the beak from Jack.

'No rudery,' said Jack. 'Behave yourself, Kiki.'

Kiki flew down to the floor, very hurt. 'Poor Kiki, poor, poor,' she muttered to herself and disappeared under the bed, where she found an old slipper and spent a pleasant half-hour pecking off a button.

Everyone talked, asked questions, laughed and felt happy. The flu was quite forgotten. But about half-past nine Lucy-Ann suddenly went pale and flopped down on the bed.

'We've overdone it!' said Bill. 'I forgot they'd all had a pretty bad time. Come on, Lucy-Ann, I'll carry you to bed! Dinah, can you walk to your room?'

Next day the doctor came as usual, and was pleased

with all four. 'Up to tea today – up after breakfast tomorrow,' he said. 'Then up the same time as usual.'

'When can they go back to school, Doctor?' asked Mrs Cunningham.

'Not yet,' said the doctor, much to the children's surprise. 'They *must* go somewhere for convalescence – ten days or a fortnight, say. Somewhere warm and sunny. This flu they've had is a bad kind – they will feel very down all winter if they don't go away somewhere. Can you manage that, Mrs Cunningham?'

'We'll see about it all right,' said Bill. 'But I'm not letting my wife go with them, Doctor. She needs a holiday herself now after so much illness in the house – and it wouldn't be much of a holiday for her to be with these four live wires. Leave it to me.'

'Right,' said the doctor. 'Well, I'll be in on Saturday, just to see that everything goes well. Goodbye!'

'A holiday!' said Dinah, as soon as the door had closed. 'I say! What a bit of luck! I thought we'd have to go straight back to school!'

There was a conference about what was best to be done. 'It's October tomorrow,' said Bill, 'and the weather forecast isn't too good. Rain and wind and fog! What a climate we have! It's a pity they can't go abroad, Allie.'

'They can't go abroad without anyone responsible in charge,' said his wife. 'We'll have to find somewhere on the south coast, and send them there.'

But all the plans were altered very suddenly and dramatically. On Friday night, very late, the telephone-bell shrilled through the house, and awoke Bill and his wife, and also Kiki, whose ears were sharper than anyone's. She imitated the bell under her breath, but didn't wake the boys. She cocked up her crest and listened. She could hear Bill speaking in a low voice on the telephone extension in his bedroom along the landing. Then there was a clink, and the little ping that sounded whenever the telephone receiver was put back into place.

'Ping!' muttered Kiki. 'Ping pong! Ping!' She put her head under her wing again, and went to sleep, perched comfortably on the edge of the mantelpiece. The children all slept peacefully, not guessing what changes in their plans that telephone call was going to mean!

In the morning Bill was not at breakfast. All the children were down, and Lucy-Ann had even got down early enough to help to lay the table. They were pale, and rather languid, but very cheerful, and looking forward now to their holiday, even though the place chosen did not seem at all exciting – a quiet little village by the sea.

'Where's Bill?' asked Dinah, in surprise at his empty place. 'I didn't hear him whistling while he was shaving. Has he gone out for an early-morning walk or something?'

'No, dear – he had to leave hurriedly in the middle of the night,' said her mother, looking depressed. 'He had a telephone call – didn't the bell wake you? Something urgent again, and Bill's advice badly needed, of course! So he took the car and shot off. He'll be back about eleven, I expect. I only hope it doesn't mean that he'll have to race off again somewhere, and disappear for weeks. It would be too bad so soon after he had come back!'

Bill returned about half-past eleven, and put the car away. He came whistling in at the side door, to be met by an avalanche of children.

'Bill! Where have you been? You haven't got to go away again, have you?' cried Dinah.

'Let me go, you limpets!' said Bill, shaking them off. 'Where's your mother, Dinah?'

'In the sitting-room,' said Dinah. 'Hurry up and talk to her. *We* want to hear your news too.'

Bill went into the sitting-room and shut the door firmly. The four children looked at one another.

'I bet he'll be sent off on another hush-hush affair,' said Jack gloomily. 'Poor Aunt Allie – just when she was looking forward to having him on a little holiday all to herself!'

Half an hour went by and the talking was still going on in the sitting-room, very low and earnest. Then the door was flung open and Bill yelled for the children.

'Where are you, kids? Come along in – we've finished our talk.'

They all trooped in, Kiki on Jack's shoulder as usual, murmuring something about 'One-two, buckle my shoe, one-shoe, buckle my two!'

'Shut up, Kiki,' said Jack. 'No interruptions, now!'

'Listen,' said Bill, when the children were all in the room and sitting down. 'I've got to go off again.'

Everyone groaned. 'Oh, *Bill*!' said Lucy-Ann. 'We were afraid of that. And you've only just come back.'

'Where are you going?' asked Jack.

'That I'm not quite sure about,' said Bill. 'But briefly – and in strict confidence, mind – I've got to go and cast an eye on a man our Government are a bit suspicious of – they don't quite know what he's up to. It may not be anything, of course – but we just want to be sure. And they want me to fly out and spend a few days round about where he is and glean a few facts.'

'Oh! So you may not be long?' said Philip.

'I don't know. Maybe three or four days, maybe a fortnight,' said Bill. 'But two things are important – one, that nobody suspects I'm out there for any Government purpose – and two, that as the climate where I'm going is warm and summery, I feel you'd better all come too!'

There was a dead silence as this sank in – then a perfect chorus of shrieks and exclamations. Lucy-Ann flung herself on Bill.

'*All* of us! Aunt Allie too! Oh, how marvellous! But how can you take us as well?'

'Well, as I told you – nobody must suspect I'm a lone investigator snooping about on my own,' said Bill. 'And therefore if I go as a family man, complete with a string of children recovering from illness, and a wife who needs a holiday, it will seem quite obvious that I can't be what I really am – someone sent out on a secret mission.'

The children gazed at him in delight. A holiday somewhere abroad – with Bill *and* his wife! Could anything be better? 'Wizard!' thought Lucy-Ann. 'I hope it's not a dream!'

'Where did you say it was? Oh, you didn't say! Do we go to a hotel? What will there be to do? It's not dangerous, is it, Bill – dangerous for *you*?'

Questions poured out, and Bill shook his head and put his hands over his ears.

'It's no good asking me anything at the moment. I've only heard the outline of the affair myself – but I did say that as a kind of camouflage I could take you all with me, and pose as a family man – and it seemed to click, so I left the High-Ups to arrange everything. Honestly, that's all I know at the moment. And don't you dare to talk about this except in whispers.'

'We won't, Bill,' Lucy-Ann assured him earnestly. 'It shall be a dead secret.'

'Secret!' yelled Kiki, catching the general excitement and dancing up and down on the table. 'Secret! High-up secret! High, high, up in the sky, wipe your feet, blow the secret!'

'Well, if anyone's going to give it away, it's Kiki!' said Bill, laughing. 'Kiki, can't you ever hold your tongue?'

Kiki couldn't, but the others could, as Bill very well knew! They hurried out of the room and up the stairs and into a little boxroom. They shut the door, and looked at each other in excitement.

'Whew!' said Philip, letting out an enormous breath. 'What a THRILL! Thank goodness for the flu! Now – let's talk about it – in whispers, please!'

3

Away they go!

That weekend was full of excitement. The telephone went continually, and finally a small, discreet car drew up in the drive on Monday night, and three men got out; they went, as instructed, to the garden door, where Bill let them in. He called to the boys.

'Philip! Jack! Go and sit in that little car out there and keep watch. I don't think anyone is likely to be about, but you never know. These are important visitors, and although we don't think anyone knows of their visit here, you may as well keep watch.'

The boys were thrilled. They crept out to the car, and sat there, hardly breathing! They kept a very sharp look-out indeed, scrutinizing every moving shadow, and stiffening every time a car came up the quiet road. The girls watched them enviously from an upstairs window, wishing they were hidden in the car too.

But nothing exciting happened at all. It was very disappointing. In fact, the boys got very tired of keeping watch, when two or three hours had gone by. They were very thankful indeed when they heard the garden door opening quietly and footsteps coming to the car.

'Nothing to report, Bill,' whispered Jack, and was just about to slip away with Philip when Kiki decided that the time had come to open her beak again. She had not been allowed to make a single sound in the car, and had sulked. Now she really let herself go!

'Police! Fetch the police! PHEEEEEEEEE!' She whistled exactly like a real police-whistle being blown, and everyone was electrified at once. Bill hadn't heard Kiki's newest achievement, and he clutched at one of the three men in alarm. All of them stood stock still and looked round in amazement.

Jack's voice came penitently out of the darkness. 'Sorry, Bill. It's only Kiki's latest. I'm awfully sorry!'

He fled indoors with Philip. Kiki, sensing his annoyance, flew off his shoulder and disappeared. She let herself down into the big waste-paper basket in the sitting-room, and sat there very quietly indeed. Outside there was the sound of an engine being revved up, and the car moved quietly out of the gateway and disappeared into the night. Bill came back indoors.

'Well!' he said, coming into the sitting-room and blinking at the bright light. 'What came over Kiki to yell for the police like that? It nearly startled us out of our wits! My word, that whistle – it went clean through my head. Where is she? I've a few straight words to say to her!'

'She's hiding somewhere,' said Jack. 'She knows she shouldn't have done that. She heard it on the radio the other night, and she keeps *on* calling for the police and doing that awful whistling. Bill, any news?'

'Yes,' said Bill, filling his pipe. 'Quite a lot. Rather nice news too – we're going to have some fun, children!'

'Really, Bill?' said his wife. 'How?'

'Well – the place we are going to – which I am not going to mention at present, in case Kiki is anywhere about, and shouts it all over the place – is quite a long way off, but as we are going by plane that won't matter. And, my dears, the Powers-That-Be have decided that they will put a small river-launch at our disposal, so that we can go on a nice little trip and see the country – enabling me to make quite a lot of enquiries on our journey!'

'It sounds great!' said Philip, his eyes shining. 'Absolutely tops! A river-launch of our own! My word, what a super holiday!'

'It does sound good,' said his mother. 'When do we go, Bill? I'll have to look out summer clothes again, you know.'

'We have to catch the plane on Wednesday night,' said Bill. 'Can you manage to be ready by then? Everything will be arranged for us at the other end – you won't have to bother about a thing.'

Everyone was in a great state of excitement at once, and began to talk nineteen to the dozen, the words almost falling over themselves. In the midst of a little pause for breath, a loud hiccup was heard.

'That's Kiki!' said Jack at once. 'She always does that when she's ashamed or embarrassed – and I bet she was horrified at her outburst in the dark garden. Where is she?'

A search began, but Kiki was not behind the thick curtains, nor under the chairs or tables. Another hiccup made everyone look about them, puzzled. 'Where *is* she? We've looked absolutely everywhere. Kiki – come out, you fathead. You haven't got hiccups – you're putting them on.'

A sad and forlorn voice spoke from the depths of the waste-paper basket. 'Poor Polly! Polly-Wolly-Olly all the day, poor Polly!' There followed a tremendous sigh.

'She's in the waste-paper basket!' cried Lucy-Ann, and ruffled all the papers there. Yes – Kiki was at the very bottom! She climbed out, her head hanging down, and walked awkwardly over the floor to Jack, climbed all the way up his foot and leg, up his body, to his shoulder.

'I suppose you've forgotten how to fly!' said Jack, amused. 'All right, you idiot – put up your crest and stop behaving like this. And DON'T shout for the police and blow that whistle any more!'

'You're going on a trip, Kiki,' said Dinah. But the parrot was still pretending to be very upset, and hid her head in Jack's collar. Nobody took any more notice of her, so she soon recovered, and began to enter into the conversation as usual.

After a while Mrs Cunningham gave a horrified exclamation. 'Do you know what the time is? Almost midnight – and these children only just recovered from being ill! What am I thinking of? They'll all be in bed again if we're not careful! Go to bed at once, children.'

They went upstairs, laughing. They had quite thrown off the miserable feeling they had had with the flu – and now that this exciting trip lay in front of them, they all felt on top of the world.

'I wonder where we're going to,' said Jack to Philip. 'Bill didn't tell us even when he thought Kiki wasn't there.'

'Bill's always cagey about everything till we're really off,' said Philip. 'It's no use badgering him – and anyway, what does it matter? It's wonderful to go off into the blue like this – literally into the blue, because we're going to fly – instead of straight back to school.'

'Lucy-Ann wouldn't like to hear me say so – but it's quite an adventure!' said Jack. 'Come on, get into bed. You must have brushed each of your teeth a hundred times.'

The next two days were very busy indeed. Summer clothes were taken from drawers and chests, canvas aeroplane-cases were thrown down from the loft by the boys, everyone hunted as usual for lost keys, and there was such a hubbub that Mrs Cunningham nearly went mad.

'Hubbub!' said Kiki, pleased with the new word, when

she heard Bill complaining about it. 'Hubbub, hip-hip-hubbub! Fetch the doctor, Hubbub!'

'Oh, Kiki – I can't help laughing at you, even though I'm so busy,' said Mrs Cunningham. 'You and your hub-bubs! You're a hubbub on your own.'

By Wednesday night all the bags were more or less neatly packed, the keys put safely in Bill's wallet, and arrangements made for someone to come in and air the house, and dust it each day. Bill went to get the car from the garage, and at last it was time to start.

Bill drove to the airport. It was exciting to arrive there at night, for the place was full of lights of all kinds. A loud amplifier was giving directions.

'Plane now arriving from Rome. Rome plane coming in.'

'The plane for Geneva will leave ten minutes late.'

'Plane arriving from Paris. Two minutes early.'

The little company, with Kiki on Jack's shoulder, sat in the waiting-room, for they were early. They began to feel sleepy in the warm room and Lucy-Ann felt her head nodding. Bill suddenly stood up.

'Here's our plane. Come on. We'll have to keep together, now. Don't let Kiki fly off your shoulder or scream or anything, Jack. Put her under your coat.'

Kiki grumbled away under Jack's coat, but as she felt a little overcome by the constant roar of arriving and departing planes, she said nothing out loud. Soon all six of them, and Kiki too, were safely in their plane-seats.

They were exceedingly comfortable, and the air hostess plied them with food and drink at once, which pleased the children immensely.

There was nothing to be seen outside the plane as it flew steadily through the night. The weather was good, the skies were clear and calm. All the children slept soundly in their tipped-back seats. Kiki, rather astonished at everything, settled under Jack's coat and went to sleep too.

The plane flew on and on. Stars faded in the sky. Dawn crept in from the east, and the sky became silver and then golden. The sun showed over the far horizon and the children awoke one by one, wondering at first where they were.

'Another two or three hours and we're there,' said Bill. 'Anyone want anything to eat? Here's our kind air hostess again.'

'I wish I *lived* on an aeroplane,' said Jack, when the air hostess brought them a tray full of most delicious food. 'Why is food always so super on a plane? Look at these enormous peaches – and I don't think I've *ever* tasted such delicious sandwiches!'

'This is fun!' said Lucy-Ann, taking her fourth sandwich. 'Jack, stop Kiki – that's her second peach, and she's spilling juice all over me!'

Yes, it was fun! *What* a bit of luck that Bill had to go on this trip!

4

What part of the world is this?

The children spent a good bit of time after that looking out of the windows and seeing the earth below. They were flying high, and very often wide stretches of white cloud, looking like fields of dazzling snow, lay below them. Then came gaps in the clouds and far down they could see hills and rivers and tiny towns or villages.

There was a great bustle when the plane at last landed on a long runway. Many men ran up, steps were wheeled here and there, luggage was unloaded, passengers streamed out of the plane and were soon greeted by friends.

A big car was waiting for Bill and his family. They were soon seated comfortably in it, and a very brown-skinned man drove them away.

'Everything laid on, you see,' said Bill. 'We are going to a fairly small place called Barira, where there is a very comfortable hotel. I don't want to stay in a large place, where someone might possibly recognize me. In fact, from now on I'm going to wear dark glasses.'

The 'small place' was a long way away, and it took the car three hours to get there. The road was very bumpy in parts, and ran through country that was sometimes very well wooded and sometimes bare and desert-like. But at last they arrived, and the big car stopped outside a rambling hotel, white-washed from top to bottom.

The hotel manager himself came to receive them, small and plump, with a very big nose. He bowed himself almost to the ground, and then barked out very sharp orders in a language the children did not understand. Porters came up and unpacked the luggage from the car, perspiring in the hot sun.

'You wish to wash, Madame?' said the hotel manager. 'Everything is most ready, and we speak a hearty welcome to you.'

He bowed them into the hotel and took them to their rooms. These were spacious and airy, and very simply furnished. The children were delighted to find a shower bath in their rooms. Jack promptly stripped and stood underneath the tepid shower.

'Any idea where we've come to, Philip?' he called. 'I know Bill said it was somewhere called Barira, but I've never heard of it in my life.'

Bill came into their room just then. 'Well, everything all right?' he said. 'Where are the girls? Oh, is that their room next to yours? Good! Ours is just across the landing if you want us. We're to have a meal in about a quarter of an hour's time. Come and bang on our door when you're ready.'

'Hey, Bill – what part of the world are we in?' called Jack. 'The men we've seen look like Arabs.'

Bill laughed. 'Don't you know where we are? Well, we're some way from the borders of Syria – a very old part of the world indeed! Tell the girls to join you as soon as they can, will you?'

The small hotel proved to be extremely comfortable. Even Kiki was made welcome, after the manager had got over the shock of seeing the parrot perched on Jack's shoulder.

'Ha – what you call him – parrot!' said the little manager. 'Pretty Poll, eh?'

'Wipe your feet,' said Kiki, much to the man's surprise. 'Shut the door!'

The small man was not sure whether to obey or not. 'Funny bird!' he said. 'He is so much clever! He spiks good. Polly, polly!'

'Polly put the kettle on,' said Kiki, and gave a screech that made the man hurry out of the room at once.

There were no other guests at the hotel. The children sat in the shade on a verandah overhung with clusters of brilliant red flowers. Enormous butterflies fluttered among them. Kiki watched these with much interest. She knew butterflies at home, but these didn't seem at all the same. She talked to herself, and the waiters going to and fro regarded her with awe. When one of them coughed, and Kiki imitated him exactly, he looked very scared and ran off quickly.

'Don't show off, Kiki,' said Jack sleepily. 'And for goodness' sake keep still. You've been dancing about on my shoulder for the last ten minutes.'

Next day plans were made for the river-trip, which was to last at least a week. Bill produced a map which showed the winding course of a river, and pointed to various places.

'We start here – that's where our launch will be. We go here first – see? And then down to this town – I don't know how you pronounce it – Ala-ou-iya – something like that. I leave you there and have a snoop round for my man – though, as I said, I might take you boys with me.'

'What's his name?' asked Jack.

'He calls himself Raya Uma,' said Bill. 'No one knows whether that is his real name or not, or exactly what nationality he is – but we do know he's a trouble-maker who wants watching. What he's out here for we simply can't imagine. It may be something that is perfectly innocent, but, knowing his record, I don't think so. Anyway, all I have to do is to spot him, find out what he's doing and report back. Nothing more – so there's no danger attached, or I wouldn't have brought you with me.'

'We wouldn't have minded if there *had* been!' said Philip. 'A spot of danger makes an adventure, you know, Bill!'

Bill laughed. 'You and your adventures! Now listen – this fellow Uma doesn't know me personally, and has never met me – but he may have been warned that his doings are being enquired about, so he may be on the look-out for a snooper. If anyone questions any of you, answer candidly at once. Say you've been ill, and this is a trip to give you sunshine, and so on – which is perfectly true as far as you're concerned.'

'Right,' said Jack. 'What's this man Uma like?'

'Here are some photographs of him,' said Bill, and he spread out five or six prints. The children looked at them, astonished.

'But – they're all of different men,' said Dinah.

'Looks like it – but they're all our friend Uma,' said Bill. 'He's a master of disguises, as you see. The only thing he cannot very well disguise is a long white scar on his right forearm, which looks very like a thin curving snake. But it's easy enough to cover that up, of course, with the sleeve of his shirt or coat, or whatever garment he happens to be wearing.'

He gathered up the prints and put them back into his wallet. 'You're not likely to recognize him at all,' he said. 'So don't go suspecting everyone you meet – you'll spoil your holiday! I know where to find people who know him, and I may get word of him. On the other hand, he may not be anywhere about now – he may have flown to America or Australia. He gads about all over the place – a most extraordinary fellow.'

Something long and sinuous suddenly glided by Bill, disappearing into the bushes nearby. He jumped, and then put out a restraining hand as Philip darted by him. 'No, Philip – that might be a *poisonous* snake – don't try any tricks with animals here.'

Dinah gave a small shriek. 'Was that a snake? Oh, how horrible! Bill, you didn't tell us there were snakes here. I hate snakes. Philip, don't you dare to catch one, else I'll scream the place down.'

'Fathead,' said Philip, sitting down again. 'All right, Bill. I won't keep a poisonous snake, I promise you. That was rather a pretty one. What was it?'

'I don't know,' said Bill. 'I'm not over keen on snakes myself. And be careful of some of the insects here too, Philip. They can give you nasty nips. Don't carry too many about in your pockets!'

Dinah was not so happy now that she knew there were snakes about. She kept her eyes on the ground wherever she walked, and jumped at the least waving of a leaf. The little hotel manager saw her and came to comfort her.

'Many snakes here, yes – beeg, beeg ones that do not bite – and little, little ones, which are much poison. The little bargua snake is the worst. Do not touch him.'

'Oh dear – what's it like?' asked poor Dinah.

'He is green with spottings,' said the manager.

'Oh! What sort of spottings?' asked Dinah.

'Red and yellow,' said the little man. 'And he is fast with his head when he strikes – *so*!' He struck out with his hand as if it were a snake darting at Dinah, and she gave a small scream and drew back.

'Ah – I fright you!' said the plump manager, filled with dismay. 'No, no, do not be fright. See, I have somethings for you!'

He scuttled off to fetch the 'somethings' and brought back a dish of extremely rich-looking sweetmeats.

'I give you my apologizings,' he said. 'And my beggings for pardon.'

Dinah couldn't help laughing. 'It's all right,' she said. 'I wasn't really frightened – you just made me jump. But thanks awfully for these sweets.'

The little man disappeared and the children tried the sweets. They were very rich, very sticky and very sweet. After one each they all felt slightly sick. Kiki, however, helped herself generously, and then began to hiccup loudly, much to the delight of a passing waiter.

'Shut up, Kiki,' said Jack. 'That's enough. Be quiet now.'

But this time Kiki really *did* have hiccups, and was rather astonished to find that she couldn't stop. 'Pardon,' she kept saying, in a surprised tone that sent the children into gales of laughter.

'That'll teach you not to be so greedy!' said Jack. 'I say – we're starting on the river-trip tomorrow! Bags I drive the launch sometimes!'

'Bags I, bags I!' repeated Kiki at once, dancing up and down. 'Three bags full! Bags I! Oh – pardon!'

Tomorrow! Away on an unknown river to mysterious places in a strange land – what could be more exciting?

5

Away down the river

Next day they all drove down to the river. The white road wound here and there, and the people they met ran to the side of the road to keep out of the way of the big car.

'They look like people out of the Bible,' said Lucy-Ann.

'Well, many of the people in the Bible came from these parts!' said Bill. 'And in some ways the people *and* their villages too have not changed a great deal, except for modern amenities that have crept in – the radio, for instance, and wrist-watches, and modern sanitation *some*-times. And cinemas, of course – you find them every-where.'

'Bill – in the picture-Bible I had years ago Abraham looked *exactly* like that man!' said Lucy-Ann, nodding towards a dignified, white-robed man walking by the roadside. 'And look at that woman with a pot on her head – pitcher, I mean. She's like the picture I had of Rebecca going to the well.'

'Hey, look – camels!' shouted Philip, suddenly excited. 'Oh, there's a baby one. I've never in my life seen a baby one before. Oh, I wish I had it for a pet.'

'Well, at least you couldn't keep it in your pocket, like a snake or a mouse,' said Dinah. 'Don't those camels look cross!'

'Yes,' said Bill. 'Camels always look annoyed. That one over there is looking down his nose at us as if he really couldn't bear the sight of our car.'

'He probably can't!' said Dinah. 'It must smell horrible to him. Yes, he does look down his nose, doesn't he? Cheer up, camel!'

They saw patient donkeys too, loaded down with such heavy pannier-baskets that it was a marvel they could walk at all. Philip was interested in the birds too, almost as much as Jack was.

'I wish I'd brought my big world-bird book,' mourned Jack. 'I'd be able to look up all these brilliant birds then. I did put it out to bring, but I left it on my dressing-table.'

'You wouldn't have been allowed in the aeroplane with that monster book,' said Bill. 'I see you brought your field-glasses, however. You'll find plenty to look at with those.'

'Is that the river?' said Dinah suddenly, as she caught sight of a flash of blue through the trees. 'Yes, it is! I say – it's very wide here, isn't it!'

So it was. The farther shore seemed quite a distance

away. Their launch was waiting for them, a trim little vessel with a boatman on board looking very spry and neat. He saluted them when they came over from the car.

The launch was beside a little jetty, and Bill looked at it with approval. He nodded to the man.

'I Tala,' said the man, and bowed. 'Tala look after ship, and look after you, Sir.'

Tala showed them over the launch. It was small but quite big enough for them all. The cabin was stuffy and hot, but nobody planned to be there very much! The bunks down below looked stuffy and hot too, but, as Bill said, they could sleep on deck, providing they rigged up a mosquito net over them. A little breeze blew every now and again, which was very pleasant.

'You start now, this minute, at once?' enquired Tala, his black eyes taking them all in. He had remarkably white teeth and a twinkle in his eyes that the children liked immediately. Bill nodded.

'Yes. Off we go. You can show me any gadgets there are, and I'll take the wheel if I want to. Cast off.'

The launch went off smoothly, her engine making very little noise. At once it seemed cooler, for the breeze was now in their faces. The children sat on the deck and watched the banks slide by on either side.

Mrs Cunningham went down into the lower part of the launch to see what kind of food was stored away there. She called to Bill.

'Just look here!' she said. 'They've done you proud

again, Bill – there's enough for an army here – and such *nice* food too! And there's a fridge packed with butter and milk. You must be quite an important person, Bill, to have all this done for you!'

Bill laughed. 'You come along up on deck and get some colour into your cheeks!' he said. 'Hallo, what are the children excited about?'

The launch was passing a small village and the village children had come out to watch it go by. They shouted and waved, and Jack and the others waved back.

'What's this river called, Tala?' asked Philip.

'It is called River of Abencha,' answered Tala, his eyes on the water ahead.

'I say, you others!' called Philip. 'He says this river's called the River of Adventure – sounds exciting, doesn't it?'

'Abencha, Abencha,' repeated Tala, but Philip thought he was trying to say 'Adventure' and not pronouncing it correctly. Tala found many English words difficult to say!

'All right, Tala – we heard you,' said Philip. 'It's a lovely name for a river, I think – the River of Adventure. Well, this is certainly an adventure for us!'

It was a quiet, peaceful trip that day, gliding along hour after hour. Bill took the wheel when Tala went down below to prepare a meal. The children wondered what kind of a meal it would be. They were all extremely hungry.

Tala came up with a marvellous repast. As Dinah said,

it was much too grand to be called just a 'meal' – it was nothing less than a 'repast', or perhaps even a 'feast'!

Tala had apparently opened a good many tins, and concocted some dishes of his own, garnished with pickles and sauces of many kinds. There were fresh rolls to go with the meal, and to follow there was fresh or tinned fruit. Lucy-Ann pounced on a big peach and put it to her lips.

'No, don't eat the skin of that peach, Lucy-Ann,' said Bill. 'All fruit eaten out here must be peeled before being eaten. Don't forget that, please.'

Mrs Cunningham really enjoyed that peaceful day, hearing the lap-lap of the water against the bows of the boat, seeing the villages slip by on the banks, and sometimes meeting other boats on the blue-green water.

The sun and wind tired them all out, and each of them fell asleep at once when they had bedded down on deck. Tala tied up the boat safely, and went to his own shake-down in the stern.

Jack just had time to think that the stars seemed amazingly large and bright before he fell fast asleep. Nobody heard a sound that night, not even the cry of a night-bird, whose voice seemed half a hoot and half a shriek. Kiki opened one eye and considered whether to answer back in her own language of squawk-and-scream – but decided that Bill might not like it!

The river was beautiful in the early morning. It was a pale milky blue, and Jack was thrilled to watch a whole covey of tiny water-birds swimming round the yacht. 'What are they?' he asked Tala, pointing to the little blue and yellow things. Tala shrugged his shoulders.

'Tala not know,' he said. Jack soon found that Tala knew absolutely nothing about birds, insects or flowers. He could not put a name to a single one. His whole interest was in the launch's engine and in the care of it.

'We come to big, big place soon,' said Tala, early that evening. He looked rather excited. 'Place name Sinny-Town.'

'Sinny-Town?' said Bill, puzzled. 'I don't think so, Tala. There is no big town along this river-side – only small ones. I've never heard of Sinny-Town. It isn't on my map.'

Tala nodded his head vigorously up and down. 'Yes, Sinny-Town. Tala know. Tala been. Half an hour and we see Sinny-Town.'

Bill took out his map, and looked down the river as it was shown there. He shook his head again, and showed the map to Tala.

'You're wrong,' he said. 'There is no Sinny-Town marked here. See.'

Tala put his finger on a place where the river shown on the map curved a little.

'Sinny-Town there,' he said. 'You will see, Sir. Tala right. Tala been there. Big, big town. Many peoples. Big, big towers, tall as the sky.'

This was most astonishing. Bill couldn't understand it.

Why wasn't this 'big, big place' shown on the map? Even small places were shown there. In fact, the little place he had planned to go to was marked as being very near the curve of the river where Tala said Sinny-Town was.

He shrugged his shoulders. Tala must be mistaken. Towers as tall as the sky – what nonsense!

The darkness came suddenly, as it always does in southern countries. Stars shone out, large and mysterious, and very, very bright. The river turned black and silver, and held as many stars as were in the sky.

'Bend of river, Sir – then Sinny-Town,' said Tala, in an excited voice. 'You will see!'

The launch glided smoothly round the bend – and then Bill and the others saw a most astonishing sight!

A great city lay there, on the west bank of the river. A city of lights and noise. A city with towers that went up to the sky, just as Tala had said!

Bill stared in the utmost astonishment. He simply could not understand it! Here was a big place not even marked on the map – and the map was a modern one, not a year old! A city could not be built in a year. Bill was more puzzled than he had ever been in his life. He stood and stared as if he could not believe his eyes.

'Tala go Sinny-Town tonight?' said Tala beseechingly. 'Tala like Sinny-Town. Tala go, Sir? Boat be all right with you, Sir.'

'Yes, yes – you go,' said Bill, finding his voice. 'Bless my soul, this is a most extraordinary thing. A large, lively town, with great buildings – and it's not marked on the map, and no one in London told me a word about it. What *can* it mean?'

'Let's visit it, Bill,' said Jack.

'Not tonight,' said Bill. 'We'll see what it looks like in the daylight. But what a brilliantly lighted place – and what enormous buildings! I simply don't understand it. It's very – very – strange!'

6

Sinny-Town

Everyone slept very well that night. They had stayed up fairly late looking at the lights of the surprising Sinny-Town. Tala had gone off in glee, leaping from the launch to the shore with one lithe spring. He had not come back by the time the others had bedded down on the cool deck, and Bill was rather uneasy, wondering if he *would* return.

But in the morning the sound of someone tinkering with the engine of the launch awoke Jack – and there was Tala, looking rather the worse for wear after his late night, at work on the plugs. He grinned at Jack when the boy stood up and stretched.

'Tala go to Sinny-Town,' he said, and nodded towards the bank. Jack remembered their surprise of the night before and ran to the other side of the launch to gaze at the mysterious Sinny-Town.

It was so extraordinary that he called to Bill. 'Bill! I say, Bill – do come and look.'

Bill awoke and joined Jack. The two of them looked at the sprawling town. Bill was astonished.

'There's something odd about it,' he said. 'Look at those towers – somehow they don't look real – and what's that over there – a palace or something? There's something peculiar about that too. Isn't one side missing? Where are your field-glasses, Jack? Lend them to me.'

Jack handed them to him and Bill gazed through them. 'No – I don't understand this,' he said, lowering them. 'The town is a most peculiar mixture of buildings – there are shacks and sheds, ancient houses, towers, that palace, and something that looks remarkably like an old temple – and here and there are crowds of people milling round, and droves of camels, and . . . no, I don't understand it.'

'Do let's go and look at it after breakfast,' said Jack.

'Yes, we certainly will,' said Bill. 'Sinny-Town is no village – it's quite a big place – but WHY isn't it marked on my map? I had a look at another map last night, but it's not shown there either. Wake the others, Jack.'

Soon they were all having breakfast. Mrs Cunningham was as surprised as the rest of them to see such a strange mixture of a town on the bank of the river.

'That palace looks quite *new*,' said Lucy-Ann, staring at it. 'And yet it must be thousands of years old and ought to be in ruins.'

After breakfast they all went ashore, leaving Tala in

charge of the launch. Kiki was on Jack's shoulder as usual, and very talkative, much to the amusement of the people they met.

'Shut the door,' she ordered imperiously. 'Fetch the doctor, Polly's got a cold. A-HOO-CHOO!'

Her sneeze was so realistic that Lucy-Ann almost offered her a hanky. Soon Jack had to make the parrot stop talking, for, on looking behind him, he found a group of small, excited children following, pointing at Kiki in delight.

They came near to the town – and then Bill gave an exclamation. 'It's not a real town! It's a fake! All these towers and temples are imitation! Look at this one – it is only a front – there's no back to it.'

They stared in wonder. Bill was right. It was just a flimsy false front, which, from a distance, looked exactly like a real temple – but behind it was nothing but boards and canvas, with joists of timber holding the whole thing up.

They went on, coming to well-built sheds, stored with masses of peculiar things, jerry-built shacks that served all sorts of purposes – one sold cigarettes, one sold soft drinks and others sold groceries and so on.

The people were a curiously mixed lot. Men and women walked or ran here and there, mostly dressed in sloppy-looking European clothes – and others, dressed in flowing robes, went on their way too. Small children with hardly anything on darted everywhere.

And then, round a corner, they came upon a curious sight. It was a procession of magnificently dressed men, walking slowly, and chanting as they went. In the midst of the procession was a space, and here, surrounded by women dressed in the robes of long, long ago, was a kind of bed on which lay a very beautiful woman, carried by four slaves, tall, strong and dark-skinned.

Bill and the others stood and stared – and then Bill heard a curious whirring noise. He looked to see what was making it – and gave an exclamation.

The others looked at him. Bill grinned at them. 'I've got it!' he said. 'I see it all now, and I can't think why it didn't dawn on me before. The reason why Sinny-Town isn't shown on the map is because it probably wasn't here when the map was drawn a year ago! See those enormous cameras? They're cine-cameras – they're taking pictures for a film, and . . .'

Then everyone exclaimed too, and began to talk excitedly.

'Of course! It's a town specially built for the making of a film of long-ago days!'

'Why didn't we think of it before! That's why that temple is only a front and nothing else!'

'And why there is such a mixture of people here!'

'*And,* of course, it's *Cine*-Town, *not* Sinny-Town as we all imagined!' said Jack. 'A town of cinema cameras taking pictures – Cine-Town.'

'It's jolly interesting!' said Philip. 'Bill, can we wander

round on our own? Look, there's a fellow doing acrobatics over there – look at him bending over backwards and catching hold of the back of his ankles with his hands!'

Bill laughed. 'All right. You can go and have a good look round. I expect this place attracts a lot of showpeople, who think they can make a bit of money by their tricks. You may see something interesting. But keep together, please. Boys, see that the girls don't get separated from you. I'll go off alone with your mother, Philip – I might pick up some useful information.'

The children knew what *that* meant! Bill hoped to find out something about Mr Raya Uma. Well, it was quite likely that he had come to Cine-Town!

They set off by themselves, followed by a little tail of interested noisy children. Beggars called to them as they passed by, holding out all kinds of wares – trays of sticky sweetmeats, covered with flies, that made the two girls shudder in disgust. Fresh fruit in baskets. Little gimcrack objects such as might be found in fairs at home. Pictures of the stars who were, presumably, acting in the film being made in the town. There were all kinds of goods, none of which the children wished to buy.

Even the babies seemed to speak English – or, rather, English with a pronounced American accent, for the company making the film was one of the biggest ones from America. It was easy to pick out the Americans and

Europeans, not only by their dress but by their bustling walk and loud voices.

The four children wandered round the false temples and towers, wondering what the film was that was being made – it was obviously a story taken from the Old Testament. Then they made their way to a large group of huts where a little crowd sat watching a man who was performing a most peculiar trick. He was walking up a ladder of knives!

A weird chant went up from two of his attendants as he climbed up the edges of the blades, setting his bare feet on them without flinching. Someone began to play a kind of tom-tom, and the children stood there, fascinated.

The man leapt down, grinning. He turned up the soles of his feet to show that they were not in the least cut. He invited the audience to come and test the sharpness of the knife-edges with their hands, and some of them did.

He beckoned to the four children and they went to the strange ladder of knives and felt the edges too – yes, they were certainly sharp! They gazed at the man in respect, and put a little money into his bag. It was English money, but he didn't seem to mind at all. He could probably change it into his own coinage at any of the ramshackle shops around.

'What a way to earn your living – climbing up sharp

knives with bare feet!' said Lucy-Ann. 'Oh, look – there's a juggler!'

The juggler was extremely clever. He had six glittering balls and sent them up and down, to and fro, as fast as he could, so that it was almost impossible for the eye to see them. He caught them so deftly that the children stood lost in admiration. Then he took six plates and juggled with those, throwing them over his shoulder and between his legs, one after the other, without dropping or breaking a single one.

Just as the children were clapping him, Jack felt a hand sliding into his shorts pocket and turned quickly. He grabbed at a small, skinny boy, but the child wriggled away quickly.

'Hey, you! Don't you dare to do that again!' yelled Jack, indignantly, feeling in his pocket. As far as he could tell, nothing had been taken – he had been too quick for the little thief. Still, it was a lesson to him and to all the others too.

'We obviously mustn't get so engrossed in watching things that we forget to guard our pockets,' said Jack. 'Why didn't *you* see that little monkey of a fellow, Kiki? You could have yelled out "Stop thief!"'

'Stopthief, stopthief, stopthief!' shouted Kiki immediately, thinking that it was all one word. This astonished all the passers-by so much that they stood and stared. One small girl darted away at once.

'She thinks Kiki is addressing *her*,' said Philip, with a

grin. 'I expect she had just planned to pinch your little bag, Lucy-Ann.'

Just then a queer, thin music floated over to them, and they stopped. 'I say – that sounds like snake-music!' said Philip, suddenly excited. 'Come on, quick – I've always wanted to see a snake-charmer at work. Quick!'

7

A surprising morning

Jack, Philip and Lucy-Ann hurried towards the sound, but Dinah hung back.

'Ugh! Snakes! *I* don't want to see them,' she said. 'I hate snakes. I'm not coming.'

'Dinah, you've got to keep with us,' said Philip impatiently. 'Bill said so. You don't need to watch, you can turn your back. But you *must* keep with us.'

'All right, all right,' said Dinah crossly. 'But why you want to go and gloat over snakes I cannot imagine. Horrible things!'

She dawdled behind, but kept within reach, and then, when they came to the little crowd surrounding the snake-charmer, she turned her back. She felt rather sick, for she had caught sight of a snake rising up from a basket, wavering to and fro. She swallowed once or twice, and felt better, but she did not dare to turn round again. She stared out over the strangely mixed crowd.

The other three were in the little crowd round the

snake-charmer. He was a rather tough-looking man, with a turban wound round his head, and a wide cloth round his middle. He had only one eye. The other was closed – but his one eye looked round piercingly, and Lucy-Ann decided that she didn't like it at all. It was as unblinking as a snake's!

Beside the man stood his attendant, a small boy, quite naked except for a cloth round his middle. He was painfully thin, and Lucy-Ann could easily count all his bony little ribs. His eyes were sharp and bright – not like a snake's, thought Lucy-Ann, but like a robin's. He was talking at top speed about the snakes in the basket.

He spoke a curious mixture of his own language and American. The children could not follow half of it, but they gathered enough to know that the snakes in the basket were dangerous ones, with a bite so poisonous that it could kill even a grown man in twelve hours.

'He dart like this,' chanted the little fellow, and made a snake-like movement with his arm, 'he bite quick, quick, quick . . .'

The man sitting by the round basket began to play again the strange, tuneless music that the children had heard a few minutes before. The snake that Dinah had seen had disappeared back into its basket – but now it arose again and everyone gasped at its wicked-looking head.

Lucy-Ann whispered to Jack. 'Jack – it's the snake that

the hotel manager told us about – green with red and yellow spots – look! What was its name now?'

'Er – bargua, I think,' said Jack, watching the snake. 'My word, it's a little beauty, but wicked-looking, isn't it? See it wavering about as if it's looking round at everyone. My goodness, here's another!'

A second snake had now uncoiled itself and was rising up slowly, seeming to look round from side to side. Some of the crowd came a little closer to the snake-charmer, and at once the small boy cried out sharply, 'Back, back, back! You want to be bit? He bite quick, quick, quick!'

The crowd at once surged back, frightened. The snake-charmer went on with his weird music, blowing interminably on his little flute, his one eye following all the movements of the crowd. A third snake arose and swayed from side to side as if in time to the music.

The small boy tapped it on the head with a stick and it sank down again.

'He very bad snake, he not safe,' explained the boy earnestly. The other two snakes still wavered about, and then, quite suddenly, the man changed his music, and it became louder and more insistent. One of the snakes swayed more quickly, and the little boy held a stick over its head as if to stop it.

The snake struck at it, and then, before anyone could stop it, slithered right out of the basket towards the crowd.

At once there were screams and howls, and everyone surged back. The small boy ran at the snake and picked it up. He threw it back into the basket, and a cry of admiration went up at once. Shouts and claps and cheers filled the air, and the snake-charmer stood up slowly, and patted the small boy on the head.

'He save you all!' he said, and then added a few rapid words in his own language. 'He brave. Snake might bite him. He brave,' he finished.

'What a kid!' said an American voice, warm with admiration. 'Here, boy – take a hold of this!' and he threw a dollar bill on the ground. The little boy darted on it as quickly as a snake, and nodded his thanks.

That was the signal for other people in the crowd to throw down money for the boy too, and he picked it all up, stuffing it into a fold of his waist-cloth.

The snake-charmer took no notice. He was busy putting the lid on the snake-basket, preparing to leave.

Jack put his hand into his pocket to throw down a coin, but to his surprise Philip stopped him. 'No, don't,' said Philip. 'It's all a fake.'

Jack looked at him in enormous surprise. 'A fake? How? That kid's as brave as can be! You heard the hotel manager tell us how poisonous those barguas are.'

'I tell you, it's a fake!' said Philip, in a low voice. 'I agree – they are barguas, and dangerous – but not one of those snakes could hurt a fly.'

'What do you mean?' asked Lucy-Ann, astonished.

'Come away and I'll tell you,' said Philip. They joined Dinah and went a little way away. Jack looked at Philip impatiently.

'Come on then – tell us how it was a fake.'

'Did you notice that when those snakes were swaying about in the basket they kept their mouths shut all the time?' said Philip. 'They didn't open them at all, or show their forked tongues, not even when one of them was tapped on the head – which would usually anger a snake and make him get ready to bite.'

'Yes – now I come to think of it, they *did* keep their mouths shut,' said Jack. 'But what does that matter? The one that escaped might easily have opened his to strike if he had had a chance. I wonder he didn't pounce at that small boy.'

'Do listen,' said Philip. 'I was a bit suspicious when I saw that those snakes didn't open their mouths at all – so that when one snake escaped – though it's my firm opinion that that "escape" was all arranged, part of the trick, you know – well, when that snake escaped and came writhing near us I took a jolly good look at him. And believe it or not, the poor thing's mouth was *sewn up*!'

The others gazed at him in horror. 'Sewn up!' said Lucy-Ann. 'Oh, how cruel! That means, of course, that the snake-charmer is perfectly safe – he can't be bitten because the snakes can't open their mouths to strike.'

'Exactly,' said Philip. 'I never knew before how the

snake-charmer's trick was done. The snake that "escaped" had its mouth well and truly sewn up – I saw the stitches. The snake was probably doped somehow, and then, while it was doped, the man sewed up its mouth.'

'But it can't eat or drink then,' said Lucy-Ann, feeling sick. 'It's cruel. Why doesn't someone do something about it?'

'That boy wasn't brave after all then,' said Jack.

'No. That's what I told you,' said Philip. 'He had been trained to put on that little bit of spectacular courage. You saw how it pulled in the money, didn't you? My word, talk about a hard-hearted swindle! To sew up snakes' mouths and use them for a living – ugh, horrible!'

'I'm jolly glad I didn't throw down any money,' said Jack.

'And I'm jolly glad I didn't watch,' said Dinah.

'I'm sorry for those snakes,' said Lucy-Ann. 'I hate to think of them.'

'So do I,' said Philip. 'Such pretty things too – that lovely bright green, and those glittering red and yellow spots. I'd like one for a pet.'

Dinah stared at him in horror. 'Philip! Don't you dare to keep a snake for a pet – especially a poisonous one.'

'Don't fly off the handle, Di,' said Jack, amused. 'You know jolly well that Bill would never allow him to keep a poisonous bargua. Cheer up!'

'Do you suppose we could buy ice-creams here?' said

Lucy-Ann, suddenly feeling that she could eat at least three. 'My mouth feels so hot and dry.'

'We'll find a decent place,' said Jack. 'What about that one over there?'

They walked over to it and looked inside. It was clean and bright, and at the little tables sat many Americans and two or three actors and actresses still in costume.

'This should be all right,' said Philip, and they went in. People stared at the children, and especially at Jack, who, of course, had Kiki on his shoulder as usual.

A little bell was on each table, so that customers could ring if they wanted anything. Jack picked up the one on his table and rang it.

'Ding dong bell,' remarked Kiki. 'Pussy's in the well. Fetch the doctor!' She went off into one of her cackles of laughter, and then began again. 'Pussy's in the well, me-ow, me-ow, puss, puss, puss! Ding dong bell!'

There was a sudden silence, and everyone stared in amazement at the parrot, who now proceeded to cough like an old sheep. Jack tapped her on the beak.

'Now then, Kiki – don't show off!'

'Great snakes!' drawled an American voice nearby. 'That's a *ree*markable parrot, young fellow! Like to sell him?'

'Of course not!' said Jack, quite indignantly. 'Shut up, Kiki. You're not giving a concert!'

But Kiki was! Delighted at all the sudden attention, she gave a most remarkable performance – and was just in the middle of it when something happened. A man came in and sat down at the children's table!

'Hallo!' he said. 'Surely I know you! Don't you belong to old Bill? Is he here with you?'

8

The snake-charmer again

The four children stared at the man in surprise. He was dressed well, and his face looked brown and healthy. He smiled at them, showing very fine teeth.

Nobody answered for a moment. Then Kiki cocked her head on one side, and spoke to the man.

'Bill! Silly-bill! Pay the bill, silly-billy, pay the billy!'

'What a wonderful parrot!' said the man, and put out his hand to ruffle Kiki's crest. She gave him a quick nip with her beak, and he scowled at once, making his face completely different.

'Well?' he said, nursing his finger and smiling again at the children. 'Have you lost your tongues? I asked you who you were with? Is it old Bill, my good old friend?'

Both girls got a quiet kick on the leg from Jack and Philip. Everyone had remembered what Bill had said. They were not to give away any information if they were asked questions!

'We're here with my mother,' said Philip. 'We've all

been ill, so this is a sort of convalescence trip. We're just having a short river-trip on a launch.'

'I see,' said the man. 'You don't know anyone called Bill then?'

'Oh yes,' said Dinah, to the horror of the two boys. 'We know Bill Hilton – is he the one you mean?'

'No,' said the man.

'Then there's Bill Jordans,' said Dinah, and by the glint in her eye the boys knew that she was making all this up. They joined in heartily.

'He may mean Bill Ponga – do you, sir?'

'Or Bill Tipps – he's the fellow who had four big cars and two small ones – is he the Bill you mean?'

'Perhaps he means Bill Kent. *You* know, Jack, the chimney-sweep Mother always has.'

'Or do you mean Bill Plonk, sir? You might know him – he's a biscuit-manufacturer, and his biscuits are . . .'

'No. I do *not* mean him – or any of the others!' said the man shortly. 'Isn't anyone called Bill with you?'

'No. As you can see, we're all alone,' said Jack.

'Where's your launch?' asked the man. This was getting awkward and Jack cast about in his mind for a way to bring the conversation to a natural end. He glanced suddenly at Lucy-Ann and spoke urgently.

'I say, old girl! Do you feel sick? Better go out, if so.'

Lucy-Ann took the cue at once and stood up, looking as ill as she could.

'Yes. Take me out,' she said, in a suitably faint voice.

The others led her down the room and out into the open air.

'Scoot!' said Philip, as soon as they were outside. 'I don't *think* he'll come after us – but he might. Jolly good idea of yours, Jack, to pretend Lucy-Ann felt sick.'

They disappeared at top speed round the building and went into an empty shed. There was a dirty window there and they peered through it, keeping a watch for the over-friendly man. Lucy-Ann made a peculiar noise.

'I think I *am* going to be sick', she said. 'Jack was right!' But she wasn't sick after all, and soon began to feel better.

'Here comes our friend,' said Jack, gazing through the dirty window. 'He's standing still, looking this way and that. Now he's got into a car – he's driving off at top speed. Goodo!'

'Do you think he was Raya Uma himself?' asked Dinah.

'Shouldn't think so,' said Jack. 'Though he did have very white teeth – did you notice? And Bill said that Raya Uma had *remarkably* white teeth. I couldn't see if he had a scar on his arm, because his coat-sleeves were long.'

'We told him about plenty of Bills,' said Dinah with a laugh.

'Bill! Pay the bill!' said Kiki, joining in as usual.

'We did, old thing!' said Jack. 'We paid for the ice-creams when they were brought to us. Didn't you notice? You're as blind as a bat!'

'Batty,' said Kiki, jigging up and down. 'Batty, batty, batty!'

'Quite right. You are!' said Philip, and everyone laughed. They went to the door of the shed. 'Is it safe to go now, do you think?' asked Dinah. Jack nodded.

'Oh yes. He won't try and get anything more out of us. He knows we were fooling with him – but he doesn't know if it was because we were being cautious, or were just plain rude. We'll have to tell Bill about it and see what he says. I think there's no doubt but that the man has got wind that someone's coming out to snoop, and has been looking out for newcomers.'

They went out of the shed and wandered round. They came to a collection of tumbledown wooden huts, which looked as if they might have been built for years, not merely for the film outfit.

'A bit too far,' said Jack. 'Let's go back. I say, though – what's that?'

A sudden cry had come to his sharp ears. He stood still and then the others heard a cry too. They also heard something even worse – the sound of a cane or stick being used as a weapon!

Every time that the sound of a blow came, there followed immediately a high-pitched scream of pain and terror.

'That's a child yelling!' said Philip. 'He sounds as if he's being half killed. Come on – I can't bear this. We've got to do something about it!'

They raced round the huts, and came to a bare space, where old boxes and crates lay about. At the back stood a man, thrashing a child with a thick stick. One or two other people were there, but nobody made the slightest attempt to stop the whipping.

'Gosh – it's that snake-charmer!' cried Jack. 'And that's the little boy who picked up the money – look, the fellow has got him on the ground!'

All four of them raced over to the angry man. Philip caught hold of his arm, and Jack wrenched the stick from his hand. The man swung round in fury.

He shouted something they didn't understand, and tried to catch at the stick. But Philip put it out of reach. 'No you don't! You're a cruel beast, lashing out at that little kid like that! What's he done?'

The man shouted again, and his one eye glittered dangerously. The small boy raised his head, and sobbed out a few words.

'He say I keep money. He say I rob. But see, I have none!'

He opened his folded waist-cloth and shook it. He pointed at the snake-charmer. 'I give him all, all! He say I spend some. He beat me. Ai, ai!'

The small boy put his thin arms across his face and wept again. The man made a move towards him as if to strike him with his bare fist, but Philip jumped forward with the stick.

'Don't you touch him again! You let him be! I shall report you for this!'

Philip had no idea to whom he should report the man, but he was determined not to let him hit the child again. The snake-charmer glared at him in fury out of his one eye. Then he made a sudden move towards his snake-basket, which lay on the ground nearby. He kicked off the lid and at once the snakes rose up, scared and angered.

'Run! Run!' he shouted, in English. 'I tell my snakes bite, bite, bite!'

Dinah turned and ran at once, but the others kept their ground. If Philip was right, and the snakes' mouths were sewn up, they were harmless, and there was no need to run. Two of the snakes came gliding rapidly over the ground towards them. Then Philip did something surprising. He threw the stick to Jack, and then knelt down on the ground. He made a curious hissing noise, the same noise that he used in his own country when he wanted to tame grass snakes.

The snakes stopped immediately. They raised their heads and looked towards the boy. Then they glided right up to Philip and ran their mouths over his hands. One snake writhed up his arm and hung itself round his neck.

The snake-charmer stared in the utmost amazement. Why – the snakes had never done that to him! They had avoided him whenever they could, for they hated him.

Never, never had he seen wild snakes go to anyone as they went to this quietly hissing boy! He wasn't even afraid!

'Snakes bite – bite, bite, bite!' he said, and stamped on the ground to frighten them and make them strike with their shut mouths.

'They can't,' said Philip scornfully, and ran his hand gently along the sides of their mouths. 'You have sewn them up. In my country you would be sent to prison for such a cruel deed.'

The man fell into a rage and yelled loudly in his own language. The small boy ran to Philip. 'Go, go! He call friends, they hurt you. Go!'

Philip put down the snakes promptly, thinking of the two girls. They must go at once if there was any danger of this fellow's friends coming and making themselves a nuisance. 'We'd better scoot,' he said to Jack. But it was too late!

Three youths had come running at the snake-charmer's call, and they surrounded the four children, pushing Dinah close to the others. Philip put on a bold face. He walked forward.

'Make way!' he said. 'Make way, or we'll get the police.'

But the youths closed in even more, and the boys felt their hearts sink. They couldn't take on these three and the angry snake-charmer too!

But Kiki was not going to stand for this kind of thing.

She danced up and down on Jack's shoulder in anger, and screamed out at the top of her voice.

'Police! Police! Fetch the police!' she screeched, and then whistled like a police-whistle. 'PHEEEEEEEEE! PHEEEEEEEEEE! PHEEEEEEEEEEEEEEEEEE!'

9

At lunch time

Kiki's shouts for the police and her marvellous imitation of a police whistle terrified all the youths. They stood aghast, staring at this extraordinary parrot. Then, with one accord, they and the snake-charmer took to their heels and fled. The snake-charmer snatched up his basket of snakes as he went – all three were in it again, which was a pity.

The four children stood gazing after the runaways, most relieved. Kiki gave an enormous chuckle, and then such a cackle of laughter that the children couldn't help joining in.

'Kiki! Thanks very much!' said Jack, scratching the delighted parrot on her head. 'I suppose you heard Philip say the word "police" and that reminded you of your police-whistle performance. Very, very lucky for us!'

'No police came, though,' said Lucy-Ann. 'Good old

Kiki! That was the best whistling you've ever done – better even than your train-whistle.'

'We'd better get back to the launch, I think,' said Philip. 'I don't like us getting mixed up in anything like this. Bill would row us like fury if something serious happened.'

They were just setting off when a small figure ran out from behind a hut. It was the little boy. He ran to Philip and took his hand. He knelt down before him.

'Take me with you, boss! Bula has gone with snakes, and I have no money. He bad man, I no like him. Take me with you.'

'I can't,' said Philip, gently undoing the boy's hands from his. 'I will give you money, though.'

'Not money. Take me with you, take Oola with you!' said the boy beseechingly.

'No, Oola, we can't,' said Philip.

'Yes, boss! Oola be yours, Oola work for you!' said the boy, clutching at Philip's hand again. 'You like snakes, boss? Oola bring you some!'

'Listen, Oola – I do like snakes – but not those with their poor mouths sewn up,' said Philip. 'And it would be dangerous to have one that could bite. Have you no family to look after you?'

'Only Bula, who my uncle is,' said Oola, still clutching Philip's hand. The boy felt really embarrassed. 'Bula bad man, Bula hit, see, see!'

He showed bruises and weals all over his body. Lucy-Ann gave a sudden little sob.

'Poor little Oola!' she said. 'Can't we take him, Philip?'

'No, Lucy-Ann, we can't,' said Philip. 'We can't collect all the poor, ill-used animals or children we see here – that mangy dog over there, the poor donkey I saw today, with sores all over it – the little baby, so thin and tiny, that we saw lying on an old rug, don't you remember? They each want help and friends – but we can't collect them all and take them to the launch. No, Oola – we cannot take you.'

'What I do? What I do?' said Oola in despair.

'We'll take you to the First Aid Tent,' said Philip. 'I saw one somewhere about. They will look after you and help you, Oola. They will bathe your bruises for you.'

Oola went with them disconsolately, dragging his bare feet, his head hanging down – but as soon as they came to the immaculately white tent, with its nurse at the door in a starched apron, Oola fled! They heard him wailing as he went, and both Dinah and Lucy-Ann had tears in their eyes as they watched the half-naked little figure running behind a shack.

'Blow!' said Jack. 'I feel awful about this. I feel as if we've let Oola down very badly – but I don't see what else we can do.'

'Come on,' said Philip. 'Let's go back to the launch.

We're supposed to be back by one, and it's almost that now.'

They made their way back to the river, none of them feeling very happy. Philip kept a watch for the man who had questioned them, but there was no sign of him. They arrived safely at the launch, and were greeted with pleasure by Tala. They all jumped aboard, and heard Bill's voice calling to them.

'You're rather late. We were getting a bit worried about you. Go and wash and we'll all have a meal.'

Over the meal they exchanged news with Bill. 'Did you find out anything about that fellow Raya Uma?' asked Philip, dropping his voice so that Tala could not hear.

'Not a thing,' said Bill. 'But perhaps I shall when I get to Ala-ou-iya. Your mother and I just wandered about, found out about this film, saw a friend we knew, and came back here. Very dull. What about you? What did you do?'

Bill sat up straight when the children began to tell him about the man in the ice-cream shop who had come up and questioned them. 'He didn't say your surname, Bill,' said Jack. 'He just kept on saying "Bill". Wouldn't he know your surname?'

'No. But he might know my Christian name,' said Bill. 'You didn't by any chance say what my surname *was*, did you?'

'Of *course* not,' said both boys indignantly. 'But we

told him a whole lot more Bills, and asked him if he meant *them*,' added Jack, with a chuckle.

'What do you mean?' said Bill, puzzled.

'Well – we asked him if he meant Bill Hilton – or Bill Jordans – or Bill Ponga – or Bill Tipps, who has four big cars and two small ones,' said Jack.

'Or Bill Kent the chimney-sweep – or Bill Plonk who makes biscuits,' went on Dinah.

Bill threw back his head and laughed. 'You little monkeys! All make-believe Bills, I gather. Well, what happened next?'

'Oh – he asked where our launch was – we'd told him about the river-trip for our convalescence,' said Philip, 'and we realized things might get a bit awkward – so Jack decided that Lucy-Ann looked as if she was going to be sick, and we shot out with her, and hid.'

Bill roared again. 'I'd rather have you kids on my side than against me,' he said. 'You're too smart for words! Well – it rather looks as if that fellow was a spy of Raya Uma's. What was he like?'

They told Bill. 'It doesn't somehow sound like Uma,' said Bill. 'Except for the teeth. No, I don't think it was Uma. If he's going about openly like that he couldn't be up to anything serious. He could be too easily watched. Still, it looks as if Uma *is* out here, if he has a friend who spots you and asks you leading questions about someone called Bill. Thanks for keeping my surname secret!'

'Any other news?' asked Mrs Cunningham. 'What else did you do?'

'Oh – the snakes!' said Dinah, remembering. 'You tell about them, Philip.'

Philip related the whole story, right down to where Kiki had yelled for the police and whistled. Bill frowned.

'Now this kind of thing won't do, you know,' he said. 'You might have got yourselves into serious trouble. You must never go wandering about in back streets again.'

'Yes, but Bill – we couldn't let that fellow go on hitting Oola without doing something about it, surely?' said Jack.

'You two boys could have gone to stop the man, and have sent the girls away for help – they would have been quite safe then,' said Bill. 'Even if your feelings run away with you, you have ALWAYS got to think of your sisters first. If you want to jump into a brawl, do it when you're alone. Understand?'

'Yes, Sir,' said both boys, rather red in the face. 'Sorry, Bill!'

'Sorry, Bill,' echoed Kiki. 'Sorry, sorry, Bill.'

Everyone laughed, and Bill changed the subject. 'That's an extraordinary place,' he said, nodding his head towards Cine-Town. 'Scores of all kinds of buildings put up just for six months! Did you see the fair they've got there?'

'No,' said the children, surprised. 'We missed that.'

'Oh yes – hoopla stalls, gambling games, dancing girls,

shooting acts and goodness knows what,' said Bill. 'I've no doubt your snake-charmer came from there. Whether he will venture back again after Kiki's alarming call for the police I very much doubt. They've even got a fire-eater there.'

'A fire-eater!' said Philip. 'I'd like to see him do his act. Take us, Bill!'

'No, I think not,' said Bill. 'I'd better be getting on to Ala-ou-iya. That's where I *really* hope to get news of Uma. You'll have to hope to see a fire-eater another time. By the way, did you see the fellow climbing a ladder of knives? We saw him just as we came back.'

'Yes, we saw him too,' said Jack. 'I do wish we had more time to spend at Cine-Town – it's ugly and strange, but it's quite fascinating!'

Bill got up, filling his pipe. He called to Tala. 'We've finished, Tala. Start for Ala-ou-iya in an hour's time, please. We should be there about six o'clock. We'll spend the night there, off-shore, of course.'

'Good, Sir!' called back Tala, and came to collect the trays. The children settled down under an awning to read. Bill had given them some books about the countryside nearby, telling them that it was extremely interesting, and that civilizations thousands of years old had lived in the countryside they passed on their way down the river.

It was a pleasant trip on the water that afternoon. Cine-Town was soon left behind as the launch glided slowly and smoothly along. Tala called to them just before six o'clock.

'We come to Ala-ou-iya!' he chanted, making the name sing on his tongue. 'You know old town, Sir? It called Ala-ou-iya, Gateway of Kings!'

10

That night

Tala took the launch deftly to a mooring-post by a small wooden jetty. One or two fishing-boats were there already. Trees came right down to the water, but beyond them the children could see the outlines of small houses, low and whitewashed. Smoke rose on the evening air, rising straight up, for there was no breeze away from the river.

'What did Tala mean – that Ala-ou-iya is the Gateway of Kings?' asked Dinah. 'It says that too in the books you gave us to read, Bill – but it doesn't explain it.'

'I don't expect it means anything much,' said Bill. 'Unless it is a name handed down from old times, when much of this country was the site of civilizations thousands of years old.'

'As old as Ur, the town in the Bible?' asked Lucy-Ann.

'Yes – as old as Ur – and probably much older!' said Bill, with a laugh. 'There must have been great palaces and temples here in this country even before the Great Flood, when Noah sailed off in his Ark.'

'Oh, "The Gateway of Kings" might *really* have meant something then,' said Dinah. 'There might have been a golden gateway leading to a palace – or to a temple. I wish this book explained more. Bill, it's strange, isn't it, to think that perhaps seven or eight thousand years ago, if we had sailed down this river, we might have passed the most wonderful buildings on the way! All towering high and glittering in the sun!'

'We might have seen the Tower of Babel, that reached to the sky,' said Lucy-Ann. 'Should we, Bill?'

'Not from this river. Babylon is miles away,' said Bill. 'Look – here comes nightfall – and out come the stars!'

'And we can see the gleam of the fires now, outside the huts, through the trees,' said Dinah. 'I love the evenings here. That little group of village houses looks most picturesque now – but I know if we went and sat near them they wouldn't look so nice. It's a pity.'

'Spitty!' said Kiki, at once. 'Spitty, spitty, spitty.'

'I didn't say that, Kiki,' said Dinah. 'I said "It's a pity." Don't be rude!'

'Spitty,' said Kiki, working herself up in a crescendo. 'Spitty, spitty, SPITTY . . .'

'Be quiet,' said Jack, and tapped her on the head.

'Spitty!' repeated Kiki at once, and went off into a shriek of laughter. Tala burst into laughter too, and his huge guffaw made them all jump. He thought Kiki was the funniest thing he had ever met, and was always bringing her titbits. He brought her one now – a piece of pineapple out of a tin. She took it in one foot, and shook the juice from it.

'Don't!' said Dinah. 'I don't like pineapple juice down my neck, Kiki. Do be good.'

'Good, good, goody good,' said Kiki, and nibbled daintily at the pineapple. 'Good boy, goodbye, good morning, good afternoon, good . . .'

Tala roared again, and Bill motioned him away. He would have stood all evening watching Kiki if he had been allowed to.

'Are you going ashore tomorrow or tonight, Bill?' asked Mrs Cunningham.

'Tonight, I think,' said Bill. 'The man I want to talk to may be out all day – and anyway I'd rather talk to him at night, with no one about.'

Bill went off about nine o'clock, slipping like a shadow through the trees. He had been told how to find the man he wanted, and any villager would direct him to the house, which was built alongside a big store.

'I think I'll turn in,' said Mrs Cunningham, after a while. 'I don't know why this air makes me feel so sleepy, but it does. You turn in too, children – and remember your mosquito-nets!'

Dinah was already yawning. She and Lucy put up their net not far from Mrs Cunningham, arranging it over their mattress on the deck. The boys were not sleepy and hung over the side of the launch, talking in whispers. Tala could be heard snoring at the other end of the boat.

'Wonder how Bill's getting on,' said Jack, in a low tone. 'Shall we wait up for him?'

'No. Better not. He may be pretty late,' said Philip. 'Let's turn in now. It must be about half-past ten. Where's our net? Oh, you've got it. Good. Come on then.'

They lay down on their mattress, glad to feel cool after the heat of the day. It was very peaceful lying there, hearing the small lappings of the river, and a night-bird calling out suddenly, or a fish jumping in the darkness.

Jack went drifting off to sleep, and began to dream of enormous palaces and golden gates, and vast store-houses of treasure. Philip tossed and turned, listening for Bill.

Ah! There he was! Philip heard a noise as if someone were creeping on to the launch, trying to keep as quiet as possible. He listened for Bill to pour a glass of lime-juice for a last drink as he always did. But no sound came. Bill must have decided to turn in at once.

Another small sound made him sit up suddenly. *Was* that Bill? Somehow it didn't sound like him. Bill was big and heavy, and no matter how quiet he tried to be, he always made *some* noise. Surely he would have made more noise than this? If it wasn't Bill – then who was it?

Philip rolled quietly off his mattress and pushed aside the mosquito-net. He sat on the bare floor of the deck and listened again. Yes – someone *was* creeping about! Someone in bare feet.

It couldn't be Tala. He had bare feet – but Philip could quite well hear his snores at the other end of the boat. Was it – was it that man who had asked them questions about Bill, come to snoop about? Or could it possibly be the snake-charmer, come for a revenge of some sort? No – that was impossible, surely!

Philip listened once more. A small sound came to him again, this time down in the cabin of the launch. He crept silently over the deck, only the stars showing him the way.

He came to the top of the hatchway steps that led down to the cabin, and listened again. Yes, someone was down there – and it sounded as if the someone was helping himself to food. And drink too! There was a noise exactly like someone drinking!

Philip thought it was probably some person from the group of houses beyond the trees. What should he do? Wake Tala? That might be a bit of a job, and Tala would probably wake up in a fright and yell, which might give the intruder time to get away!

Then a bright thought came to Philip. Of course – he could close the hatchway and catch the thief that way! So he tried to shut it down, but it was tightly fastened back, and he couldn't move it. He decided to creep back to Jack and wake him. Together they would be a match for any native.

He crept back very quietly, stopping every now and again to listen for any other sounds from the intruder. He half thought he heard one behind him and listened again. No. Nothing.

On he went, and rounded the corner that led to his mattress, coming out of the shadow into the starlight.

And then he saw a black shadow standing in front of him! A shadow that seemed to look at him and recognize him. It flung itself on him, and held him tightly, while he struggled to shake it off.

'Boss!' said the shadow. 'Boss, Oola follow you. Oola here, boss. Oola here!'

The sound of Oola's voice woke everyone up – everyone, that is, except the snoring Tala. Mrs Cunningham sat up at once. Jack leapt off his mattress and found himself entangled in his mosquito-net. The girls sat up with hearts thumping loudly. What was happening?

Jack switched on a torch, and Dinah felt about for hers. Mrs Cunningham threw aside her net, and flashed her own torch in the direction of the noise. It lighted up a queer sight!

Philip was standing on the deck, and little Oola was kneeling in front of him, his arms clasping Philip's knees so tightly that the boy couldn't move!

'Let go!' said Philip. 'You're waking everyone up. What on *earth* have you come here for?'

'Oola yours, boss,' said the small voice. 'Oola belong you. Not send Oola away.'

'Philip! What *is* all this?' called Mrs Cunningham. 'Where's Bill? Isn't he back yet?'

'No, Mother!' said Philip. 'This is the kid we rescued from that snake-charmer we told you about – the one who was beating him. He's followed us all the way here!'

'Oola follow boat, all way, all way, Oola run,' said Oola.

'Good gracious! Fancy running all the way down the banks of the river!' said Jack. 'Poor little creature! He seems determined to be near you, Philip. Oola, are you hungry?'

'Oola eat down there,' said the little boy, pointing towards the hatchway. 'Oola no food two, three days.'

Mrs Cunningham examined him by the light of her torch, and exclaimed in horror. 'Why, he's absolutely *covered* in bruises and weals – and he's as thin as a rake. Poor little thing! Has he *really* run all the way after the boat to find you, Philip?'

'Seems so,' said Philip, finding his heart suddenly full of pity and affection for this strange little creature. He couldn't bear to think of him clambering through the bushes by the riverside all day long, trying to follow the boat – hungry, thirsty, tired and sore. All because Philip had rescued him from his hateful uncle! Perhaps nobody had ever been kind to him before.

Suddenly a voice came from the bank. 'Hallo! Are you all still up? I hope you didn't wait for me.'

It was Bill. He leapt on to the launch, saw Oola kneeling on the deck and stopped in amazement.

'Whatever's all this? What's happening?' he demanded. 'Who's this come to visit us in the middle of the night?'

11

Oola and his present

Oola crouched down at the sound of Bill's loud voice. Philip felt him trembling against his knees. He pulled him up. 'It's all right,' he said. 'Don't be frightened. Bill, this is that kid we rescued this morning from the snake-charmer. He's followed us all the way here, running along the banks.'

Bill stared in astonishment. 'But – he can't do this!' he said. 'Climbing on board someone else's boat in the middle of the night! Has he stolen anything? Some small kids are taught to steal as soon as they can walk.'

'He took some food from the cabin. He says he hasn't had any for two or three days,' said Lucy-Ann. 'Bill, he seems to think he wants to be Philip's servant. Whatever are we to do?'

'He'll have to go,' said Bill. 'It's just a trick to get on the boat. No doubt his snake-charmer uncle has put him up to this, and is waiting for his share of the goods! Clear off, now, boy! Quick!'

Oola was so scared that he could hardly walk. He left Philip and stumbled over the deck towards the jetty. As he passed Mrs Cunningham, she put out her hand to the stumbling boy, and caught him, so that he came to a standstill. She turned him round gently so that he stood in the light of her torch, with his back towards Bill.

'Bill – look!' she said. And Bill looked, and saw the poor thin little body, with the bruises all over it. He gave an exclamation.

'Good heavens! Who did that? Poor little creature, he looks half-starved. Come here, Oola.'

Oola came, half reassured by the kinder tone in Bill's voice. Bill shone his torch on him, and the boy blinked. 'Why did you come, Oola?' asked Bill, still stern. 'Tell me the truth and nothing will harm you.'

'I come to find *him*,' said Oola, and pointed to Philip. 'I make him my boss. Oola his servant. Oola bring present for boss.'

Bill looked him over. Except for the dirty cloth round his waist, Oola had nothing to bring!

'You bring no present,' said Bill. 'Why do you lie, Oola?'

'Oola spik truth,' said the boy. 'My boss, he say he like snake. Very much like snake. So Oola bring one. Bargua snake!'

And, to everyone's horror, Oola slid his hand into his waist-cloth and brought out a slim, wriggling green snake, spotted with bright red and yellow!

'Its mouth isn't sewn up!' yelled Jack. 'Look out, every-body! Look out, Oola, you fathead! It's a poisonous snake. Its bite will kill you!'

Dinah shot to the hatchway, ran down and locked her-self into a cupboard, trembling all over. A *bargua*! One of the most poisonous snakes there were! How COULD Oola wear it round him like a belt! She felt quite sick.

Oola still held the snake, which writhed about in his hand, opening its mouth and showing its forked tongue.

'Throw it overboard, Oola!' shouted Bill. 'For good-ness' sake, throw it overboard! Are you mad?'

'Oola bring present for boss,' said Oola obstinately. He lifted the snake towards Philip, who retreated at once. He liked snakes. He was not afraid of them. But to take hold of a poisonous one which was already frightened and full of anger would be a crazy thing to do!

'THROW IT OVERBOARD!' yelled Bill, terribly afraid that somebody would get bitten. 'You silly little idiot!'

'Snake not bite,' said Oola. 'All poison gone. See!'

To everyone's horror he forced open the snake's mouth. Philip bent down and looked inside, suddenly feeling that the snake might not be dangerous after all. He looked for the poison-gland and the duct that led down to the hollow tooth out of which poison pours when a snake bites.

He looked up again in the midst of a dead silence. 'The snake's *not* poisonous,' he said, and he calmly took it from Oola. 'Someone has cut the ducts that take the poison from the poison-glands to the teeth. It's a horrible trick, because it usually means that the snake dies in three or four weeks' time. Oola – who did this?'

'Old woman,' said Oola. 'Oola tell her my boss wants bargua snake, and she give Oola this one. Safe snake, boss, not like snake-mouth sewn up. You like this one?'

Philip was now talking to the snake in his special 'animal' voice, and it was attending, lying quite still in his hands.

'Poor thing!' said Philip. 'All because of me you have been injured! You have no poison in you now, but you will die because of that. You shall live with me and be happy till then. Oola, you must never have such a thing done to snakes again! It's cruel!'

'Yes, boss,' said Oola humbly. He looked round fearfully at Bill. 'Oola stay?' he enquired. 'Oola boss's man. Belong him,' and he pointed at Philip.

'All right – you can stay for the night anyhow,' said Bill, feeling quite exhausted with all this. 'Come with me. I'll wake Tala and you can sleep with him.'

'Go, Oola,' said Philip, seeing the boy hesitate, and Oola went.

'I wanted to put some ointment on his back,' said Mrs Cunningham. 'Poor little mite! Oh, Philip – have we *got* to have that snake living with us now?'

'I'll keep it in my pocket,' said Philip. 'I won't let it out unless I'm alone, or with Jack. It's quite harmless, Mother.

Mother, can we let Oola stay with us? He can help Tala and I'll see that he's not a nuisance. I can't imagine why he has attached himself to me.'

'Well, you rescued him from that awful uncle of his, didn't you!' said Lucy-Ann.

'We'll see what Bill says,' said Mrs Cunningham. 'He'll do what he can for him, I know. Where's Dinah?'

'Probably locked in the broom cupboard!' said Jack. 'I'll go and see.'

Dinah was still in the cupboard, feeling rather ashamed of herself now, but not daring to come out till someone fetched her. She was most relieved to see Jack.

Jack decided not to tell her yet that Philip had the snake. She might kick up a terrible fuss and have a violent quarrel with Philip. Better have all that in the morning, not now, when everyone was tired and upset.

'Come on out, Di,' he said, opening the door. 'Don't worry! The snake wasn't even poisonous! The poor thing has had its poison-ducts cut, so no poison can run down to the hollow fangs. We had all that fright for nothing.'

'I don't believe it,' said Dinah. 'It's still poisonous. You're just making that up to get me out!'

'No. It's true, Dinah!' said Jack. 'Do come out. Everybody wants to go to bed now. Oola has gone to sleep with Tala. He's absolutely determined to be Philip's servant, poor little boy!'

Dinah imagined that the snake had also gone with Oola, and she consented to come up on deck again. Soon everyone had settled under their mosquito-nets and were soon asleep. What an extraordinary evening!

In about half an hour, when Tala was snoring loudly again, a small figure crept over the launch to where the boys slept. It was Oola. He had come to be near his 'boss'! He curled himself up on the bare deck at Philip's feet, and closed his eyes, perfectly happy and at peace. He was with his 'boss'. He was guarding him! No one could come near Philip without waking Oola.

In the morning Tala, as usual, awoke first. He remembered the episodes of the night and looked for Oola. The boy was gone. He nodded his head in satisfaction. Had he not told Mister Bill that boys like that were no good? But Mister Bill had said, 'He sleeps with you, he will stay here.' And now the boy was gone, and Tala was right.

He prepared breakfast, planning what to say to Bill. 'Sir, Tala right. Tala spoke true. Boy gone.'

Tala was therefore extremely surprised and disappointed to see Oola curled up at Philip's feet. He gave him a push with his foot and Oola was up on his feet at once, ready to defend Philip.

'You go back there,' said Tala fiercely, in his own language, but under his breath so as not to wake anyone. He nodded towards his own quarters. Oola shook his head and sat down by Philip again. Tala raised his hand as if to strike him and Oola slid away deftly, running to hide.

But as soon as Tala went away Oola came back to Philip again, and sat looking down at the sleeping boy with so much pride and admiration in his face that Philip would have been quite embarrassed to see it.

The snake was safely in a little basket beside him. Oola scratched his finger against the basket and whistled very softly. The snake hissed and tried to get out.

'You are my boss's snake,' Oola told it, in his own language. 'You belong him, Oola belong him!'

What a to-do at breakfast when Dinah realized that the snake now belonged to Philip, and he was going to keep it. She gave such a shriek when its head peeped out of his pocket that everyone jumped. 'Philip! I won't have you keep that snake. You know how I hate snakes. Bill, tell him he mustn't. Bill, I do so hate them. I shan't stay a minute longer on this boat if you say he can keep it. I'll go back to the hotel!'

'All right, Dinah,' said Bill mildly. 'There's no need to go up in smoke. I shan't stop you from going back to the hotel if you are so distressed. I'll get Tala to run you back with a note to the hotel manager. You should be quite all right there, especially as he has two nice old English ladies coming to stay at his hotel this week to do some painting. They'll look after you.'

Dinah couldn't believe her ears. What! Bill would actually let her go back – all alone – instead of ordering Philip not to keep the snake?

'I'll call Tala now, shall I?' said Bill.

Dinah went brilliant red, and looked at him with tears

in her eyes. 'No,' she said. 'I'd – I'd rather put up with the snake than leave you all. You know that. You win, Bill.'

'Good girl, Dinah,' said Bill, with a sudden smile. 'Now – what are our plans for today? And WHAT are we going to do with Oola?'

12

Good news for Oola

Oola had been sent to have breakfast with Tala. Tala was very offhand with him, and kept him strictly in his place. He liked children, but this boy had no business here, on *his* boat, thought Tala.

Oola did his best to please Tala. He listened to all that he had to say, only spoke when he was spoken to, and put himself at the man's beck and call, running here and there at top speed for him.

When Tala was tinkering with the engine, Oola crept away to see Philip. He sat down in a corner and feasted his eyes on the boy, noting the tuft of hair in front, just like Dinah's, the loud, merry laugh and the way he waited on his mother.

Oola nodded in satisfaction. This was his 'boss'; never before had he met anyone to whom he wanted to give such utter loyalty or love. He had never known his mother, who had died when he was born, and he had hated his father, who was as cruel as Bula, his uncle.

When his father had gone away he had given the boy to Bula, to be of use to him in his snake-charming.

And then had begun a miserable life for Oola, which had become steadily worse. But now – ah, now he had *chosen* a master, his 'boss' Philip, the boy who sat over yonder, listening to big Mister Bill. Oola patted his full stomach contentedly, and thought about the present he had given to his 'boss'. Philip had the snake in his pocket – or somewhere about him – yes, under his shirt. Oola could see the boy put his hand there at times as if he were caressing something.

He heard his name being spoken by Bill, who was just then saying, 'And WHAT are we going to do with Oola?'

Oola's heart nearly stopped beating. To do with him? What did Big Mister Bill mean? Would they throw him overboard – or give him to the police? He bent forward anxiously to listen – and just at that moment a strong brown hand came down, and yanked him upright by the neck.

It was Tala! 'What are you doing here?' he said, in his own language. 'Sitting here half asleep in the morning! You come and help me, you lazy little son of a tortoise!'

Oola gazed at him fiercely, but did not dare to disobey. The words Bill had said rang in his ears still. '*What* are we to do with Oola?'

Bill and the others were discussing everything. Bill was all for putting the boy ashore, giving him some money and letting him go off to some relative. How could they bother with a boy like that on the boat?

Mrs Cunningham wanted him to have a chance. 'At least let him stay till we've fed him up a bit and put some flesh on him,' she said. 'He's such a miserable little specimen. And when he looks up at me with those big frightened eyes as if all he expects is a blow, I just can't bear it.'

'He'd be an awful nuisance to Philip,' said Bill. 'I know what it is when one of these kids takes a fancy to anyone. Philip would find him underfoot all the time!'

'I could deal with him,' said Philip quietly. 'I wouldn't mind.'

'What do you others think?' asked Mrs Cunningham, looking round.

'We'd like him,' said Lucy-Ann, and everyone nodded. 'We'll keep him busy – and so will Tala! Once Tala has got used to him he'll like him, I know he will. Don't send him away, Bill.'

Dinah was sitting as far away from Philip as she could, trying not to think of the snake he had somewhere about his person. She still felt very upset but she was doing her best to be sensible. Bill felt pleased with her. He turned to her.

'You agree too, Dinah?'

She nodded. 'Yes. I wish he was cleaner and not so skinny, but I like him.'

'Oh, well – we can soon get rid of the dirt and the

bones, said Bill. 'I'll give him a trial, and tell Tala to see that Oola washes himself, and has a clean bit of cloth to wind round his middle. I'll call Oola. OOLA! OOLA!'

Oola dropped the piece of wire he had been holding while Tala tinkered with the engine and ran forward immediately, his heart thumping. Was he to be turned away?

He stood before Bill, eyes downcast. 'Oola,' said Bill, 'we are going to give you a chance and let you stay with us while we are on this ship. You will do everything that Tala tells you. I am Big Mister Bill, he is Little Mister Tala. Understand?'

'Big Mister kind, Big Mister good!' said Oola, his eyes shining. 'Oola glad. Oola be good worker!'

He looked at Philip, his face one big smile. 'I be with my boss!' he said to him. 'Oola boss's servant! Oola work for him!'

Bill called Tala. 'Tala! Come here a minute!' Tala came so quickly that it was quite obvious he had been listening. He saluted and stood waiting, his face rather stern.

'Tala – Oola is to stay with us while we are on the ship. See that he washes himself and eats properly. See that he does not steal. Give him work to do. Tell me if he is good or bad.'

Tala saluted again but said nothing. He sent a quick look at Oola, who was now standing as close to Philip as possible, his head bowed, listening.

'That's all, Tala,' said Bill. 'Today we go on down the river, and I will tell you where to stop.'

'Very good, Sir,' said Tala, and went off, still looking rather grim. He heard his name called again.

'Tala! Tala, Tala, Tala!' He went running back at once. But this time the caller was Kiki, who felt that she could not keep silent any longer!

'Tala! Wipe your feet! One, two, four, seven, three, quick march! PHEEEEEEEEEEEE!'

The police-whistle ending startled everybody, especially Oola, who almost threw himself overboard in his fright. Tala forgot his gloom and burst into one of his enormous guffaws, staggering about the deck in delight at the parrot's ridiculous talk.

'Stop that whistling, Kiki,' ordered Mrs Cunningham. 'It goes right through my head. What a din!'

'Din-din-din-dinner!' chanted Kiki, enjoying the interest she had created. 'Din-din-din . . .'

But a sharp tap on her beak from Jack silenced her, and she flew to a corner and muttered rude things all to herself.

'Tala, take Oola with you and deal with him,' said Bill. 'See that he gets clean from top to toe first of all. He's dirty.'

This was news to Tala. He hadn't realized that Oola was dirty from his journey. He looked in his direction at once and pretended that he could see something horrid. He wrinkled up his nose in disdain.

'Bad,' he said scornfully. 'Bad dirt. Pooh!'

'Pooh!' repeated Kiki in delight, waddling out of her corner. 'Pooh! Boo! Bad dirt, pooh!'

Tala roared, grabbed Oola by the hand and went off with him, Oola protesting all the way.

When they were safely out of hearing, Jack turned to Bill.

'Did anything interesting happen last night?' he asked. 'At Ala-ou-iya, I mean. You were jolly late back, weren't you?'

'Yes. I don't know that I found out much,' said Bill. 'The man I had to contact didn't come home to his house till fairly late, and I had to wait for him. He knows Raya Uma, of course, and he thinks he is up to something, because he keeps disappearing, but nobody knows where he goes.'

'What is Uma supposed to be doing when he isn't disappearing?' asked Mrs Cunningham.

'Well, apparently he is interested in Cine-Town,' said Bill. 'He goes there quite a lot – has a bedroom in the big hotel they've run up there. He says he was an actor himself once, and is extremely interested in films – that may be just a tale, of course, to cover other activities.'

'Yes – but I can quite well believe that he *was* once an actor,' said Mrs Cunningham. 'Those photographs you have of him – they might all be of different men! I am sure he could put on different voices and ways with each change of costume!'

'You're right,' said Bill. 'Well, granted that he *was* once an actor, and *is* interested in films, where does he disappear to for a week or ten days every now and again? He's up to mischief of some kind, I'm sure!'

There was a pause. 'What *sort* of mischief, Bill?' said Jack.

'Well – here is a list of some of his past activities,' said Bill, taking out a notebook. 'Gun-running on a big scale – that means supplying guns illegally to those who will pay a big price for them. Spying – he's clever at that, but no Government will use him now, because they can't trust him – he's quite likely to go over to the other side if they offer him a bit more.'

'What a charming fellow!' said Jack, stroking Kiki, who was now on his knee.

'And smuggling,' said Bill. 'That's another thing he is very successful at. He did it on such a big scale once that he almost made himself a millionaire – then someone gave him away, and in spite of big bribes he offered to others to take the blame, he had to go to prison. Well – those are just a few things he has done. Now it's said that he has very little money indeed, not many friends and is determined to pull off something big.'

'And you think that something big might be hatched out here?' said Philip. 'How can you stop him?'

'It isn't my job to stop him – only to report back to headquarters,' said Bill. 'If it's nothing that will harm our own country or its trade, they won't do anything, but if he's stirring up trouble somewhere – arming some group or other that will start a small war and plunge us all into danger once more, then we *shall* have something to say.'

'And you found out nothing much last night?' said Mrs Cunningham. 'Well, maybe you'll track down something at the next place – what was its name?'

'A place called Ullabaid,' said Bill. 'The man I saw yesterday says that Uma has a small motor-boat himself, and uses this river quite a bit – so it's clear that the places he goes to are somewhere on or near the river. Well – we'd better start. Go and see if Tala is ready, Jack. Tell him we'll go slowly – it's a lovely day, and we're in no hurry!'

Jack hurried off to the other end of the boat.

'Can you start again now, Tala?' he called. 'You can? Good! Off we go then!'

13

After tea

It was a lovely trip that day. The sun as usual shone all day long, and Tala kept near to the left bank on which tall trees grew, in order to have a little shade when possible. They passed many villages on the banks, and whenever the natives saw the boat gliding along, out they came and shouted and waved.

Oola was kept busy by Tala, and Philip saw little of him till the afternoon rest. The sun was so hot then that the boat was run in under the shade of trees, and moored. Everyone puffed and blew, and Bill ordered a general rest.

Then it was that Oola crept forward to where the boys lay in a shady corner, and curled up not far off, his eyes on Philip.

Philip saw him and grinned at him, and Oola was happy at once. 'Boss,' he whispered, 'Oola is here to guard you. Sleep in peace!'

And, although everyone else on board, including Tala, slept soundly, Oola was awake, his eyes darting about at any sound, but always coming back to rest adoringly on Philip's flushed face. Once he saw the wicked-looking head of the bargua snake peeping out of the boy's shirt, and smiled proudly. Ah – his lord had his present safely. He even kept it close to his heart.

Tea was a very pleasant meal. Everyone felt refreshed after their sleep, and was ready for biscuits and something to drink. Mrs Cunningham was the only one who wanted a cup of tea – the others all demanded lime-juice.

Oola had disappeared as soon as he heard Tala calling for him in a fierce whisper. Tala was actually quite pleased with the small boy – but he was jealous of the way he went to sit near the children when he had a chance. Tala would not have dared to do that.

Oola had become extremely interested in the launch's motor. Tala was already amazed at the way the boy grasped all the details. 'Oola drive boat!' said the boy, after tea. 'Oola know how!'

'Oh no you don't,' said Tala at once. 'No monkey tricks from you, Oola, or I go straight to Big Mister Bill and say "Throw this boy overboard, he no good, Sir!" You hear, Oola?'

'I hear, Little Master,' said Oola at once, terrified that Tala might complain of him. 'Oola clean up oil for you? Oola polish?'

Yes – Oola was welcome to do any of the dirty work, certainly. The only thing that Tala regretted about that was that the boy would become filthy dirty again – and

Tala had taken great pride in getting him spotlessly clean that morning. He had rubbed far too hard, and the boy had cried out when his bruises had been roughly scrubbed.

'Ah – no filth, now, no dirt!' said Tala, when he had finished. 'You had much dirt, Oola, very, very bad.'

Oola certainly looked better now – clean, his mass of black hair smoothed back, and a new, brilliant blue cloth round his middle, of which he was extremely proud.

They came to Ullabaid, a pleasant-looking village set a little back from the bank of the river. There was quite a fleet of small boats tied to the fairly big jetty.

'I'm going ashore,' said Bill. 'Like to come with me? We'll leave your mother in peace, I think. We're a noisy lot, you know!'

The children leapt to the jetty with Bill and ran ashore, leaving Tala, Oola and Mrs Cunningham behind. Tala was annoyed, because he would have liked to stretch his legs ashore too, and because he could not go he would not let Oola go, either, and set him a long job to do. Oola scowled, determined to slip off as soon as Tala's back was turned – or, as was most likely, the man fell asleep. He had the unusual gift of being able to sleep at any moment, and in any place, no matter how uncomfortable.

The village of Ullabaid was quite a big one. There were the usual low, whitewashed houses, with sleeping-roofs, and the usual hearths outside for cooking. There

were also the crowds of almost-naked small village children, first half afraid and shy, then bold and curious.

Bill went to the biggest house in the place, which
turned out to be a school. The teacher was friendly, with
a fine face, intelligent and kind. He seemed surprised to
see Bill, but when Bill showed him a card, and spoke a
few words in a low tone, he asked him in at once.

The four were left to wander round. Kiki was quite
silent for once in a way, staring round at the big-eyed
children of the village.

A boy about twelve came up with a packet of post-
cards in his hands. He showed one to Jack, and pointed
away in the distance, nodding his head vigorously, and
saying something over and over again.

The four children crowded round to look at the card.
It was a picture of a ruin – an old, old temple which had
apparently been discovered and excavated some years
before when a famous archaeologist had brought along a
big digging-party.

'The Temple of the Goddess Hannar,' read Philip.
'Looks interesting. Shall we go and see it while Bill is
busy? Here, boy – how far is it? How – far?'

The boy could not speak any English, but he guessed
what Philip was saying, and gestured that he would take
them.

They followed the boy between the trees and then
through some cultivated fields, and were themselves

followed by a rabble of excited children, who could see that a tip would soon be forthcoming.

And behind the rabble came a small figure, keeping out of sight – Oola! He had waited till Tala had fallen asleep, and had left the launch immediately. He had asked where his friends had gone, and been told – and now he was keeping them in sight, not daring to join them.

The rabble of children began to push close to the four friends, and Jack looked round impatiently. 'Keep back!' he said. 'Do you hear me? – keep back!'

But after a moment or two the little crowd was on their heels again – and this time Kiki took a hand.

'Back!' she ordered. 'Back, back, quack, quack, BACK!' And then she gave her famous imitation of an aeroplane about to crash, which alarmed the little crowd behind so much that they at once kept a very long distance away.

Philip laughed. 'Good old Kiki!' he said. 'I don't know what we'd do without you!'

They came to the temple at last. It was rather disappointing – much more of a ruin than the picture appeared to show. 'It's like one of those buildings in Cine-Town,' said Lucy-Ann. 'All front but not much at the back!'

'Look here,' said Philip suddenly. 'See these funny little insects, basking in the sun – I think my snake would like those. He's probably hungry by now.'

And, to Dinah's horror, Philip slid the bargua snake from beneath his shirt, and let him loose on the ground, not far from the insects.

Dina screamed, of course, and ran back. Her scream startled the local children – and when they saw the snake, which they all knew to be deadly poisonous, they too screamed in terror and fled.

'Bargua!' they shouted. 'Bargua!' The big ones dragged along the little ones, and even the big boy who was the guide fled too, after one look at the gliding snake.

'Good gracious!' said Philip, quite as startled as the other children. 'They've all gone – just because I took my snake out for a meal. What a to-do!'

'I don't blame them,' said Dinah, from a distance. '*We* know the snake's safe – but they don't! Honestly, Philip, that was a mad thing to do. Anyway, you'll lose the snake now, thank goodness! It won't come back to you now you've let it loose.'

'Well, if it doesn't, it can go,' said Philip. 'But I bet it'll come back!'

The snake snapped at the insects, and had a very good meal. It also glided into some undergrowth and caught a small frog, which it swallowed whole. Then it came back to Philip! The others watched in amazement as it glided over to him, and, without any hesitation at all, wriggled up his leg, made its way between two buttons of his shirt and disappeared.

'Ugh! It makes me feel sick,' said Dinah, watching in fascinated horror.

'Don't watch then, silly,' said Philip. Then he looked round, alarmed.

'I say – I believe it's going to get dark pretty soon – what's the time? Whew, yes, we've let the time slip by without noticing it. We must get back to the launch at once. Come on.'

But after about ten minutes the children knew they had gone wrong. They stopped and looked round.

'We didn't pass that tree struck by lightning before, did we?' said Jack doubtfully. 'Anyone remember it?'

Nobody did. 'Better go back a bit,' said Philip, feeling anxious. 'Buck up. Darkness may come at any moment and none of us has a torch.'

They went back for a hundred yards or so, and then took another path. But this one led them into a wood and they knew *that* was wrong. They went back again, all of them in rather a panic.

'I'll shout and see if those local children will come back,' said Jack. So he called in a stentorian voice: 'Hey, you kids! Come back! Come back, I say!'

'Come back, I say!' echoed Kiki, and ended with a screech that could surely have been heard half a mile away.

But no little band of local children came running up. Except for a bird that went on and on singing without a stop, there was hardly a sound to be heard.

'What are we to do?' said Jack anxiously. 'There isn't even a house in sight. Gosh, this is awful, Philip!'

'What I'm afraid of is that darkness will fall suddenly, as it always does here,' said Philip.

And, just as he said that, darkness did fall, like a black curtain! Now they were truly lost, and Lucy-Ann caught hold of Jack's hand in fright.

'What are we to do?' she said. 'What are we to do?'

14

Back to the boat

The four children stood in the darkness, hoping to see the stars shine out bright and clear. Then they might be able to see a little. But for once in a way it was a cloudy night, and only when the clouds parted could a few stars be seen.

Their eyes got used to the darkness in a little while, and they made a few steps forward. Then Jack thought he caught sight of something moving cautiously a short distance away.

'Who's there?' he called at once. 'Don't come any nearer. Who is it?'

The shadow moved quickly forward, and knelt down at Philip's feet. He felt two hands grasping his knees. It was Oola!

'Oola here, boss,' said a voice. 'Oola follow, follow. Tala say no, not come, but Oola come. Oola guard you, boss.'

Such a wave of relief went over all four children that they could hardly speak!

'*Oola!* Good gracious, you're the last person we expected,' said Philip gladly. He patted the boy's head as he knelt. 'Get up. We're VERY glad to see you. We're lost. Do you know the way back to the launch?'

'Yes, boss,' said Oola, delighted at the pat on his head. 'Oola take you now. Follow Oola.'

'Have you been behind us all the time, Oola?' asked Lucy-Ann, astonished.

'Yes, Missy, all time Oola follow, follow,' said Oola, walking on ahead. 'Oola guard his boss.'

Oola seemed to have cat's eyes. He went forward without any hesitation, taking this path and that, and at last they came to the village, which now had fires alight, and looked rather mysterious.

The band of children came running up when they saw strangers walking through their village – but when they saw that it was the same children who had had the terrible snake, they ran away in fear, crying out loudly, 'Bargua! Bargua!'

Philip stopped. He had seen the big boy who had acted as guide. He was standing some distance away, peering at them, lighted by the flames from a fire.

'Oola – see that boy over there?' said Philip, pointing. 'Go give him this money.'

'No! Boy not good!' said Oola indignantly.

'Oola, yes!' said Philip, in a commanding voice, and

Oola at once took the money and sped off to the boy. Judging by his angry voice, he was ticking the boy off well and truly – but he gave him the money all the same. The boy was delighted and ran into his house at once, calling out something in an excited voice.

'After all, the kid *did* take us all the way to the old temple,' said Philip, and the others agreed. 'Whew! What a stir the snake made! I never dreamed that those kids would be so frightened.'

'We're going to get into a frightful row with Bill when we get back to the launch,' said Jack gloomily. 'He won't like us being out in the dark like this.'

'Let's hope he won't be back,' said Dinah, who had no wish to make Bill annoyed again.

They made their way quickly to the river, and went on board the launch. Mrs Cunningham was sitting reading down in the cabin, for it was unexpectedly cool that evening. She was most relieved to see them.

'Oh – you had Oola with you – that's all right then,' she said, as she saw Oola's face peering down the hatch with the others. 'Bill's not back yet. Are you hungry? Because if so, tell Tala, and we'll have supper.'

'We're always hungry,' said Jack. 'You never really need to ask us that, Aunt Allie. But we'd better wait for Bill.'

Bill came back ten minutes later. 'Had supper yet?' he asked. 'Good, tell Tala we'll have it. I'm famished. Well, what did you four do?'

'Nothing much – just went to see an old temple, but

there wasn't much to look at when we got there,' said Jack.

'There was a lot of digging round about this district some years ago,' said Bill. 'I've been hearing about it from that teacher you saw – a very fine and intelligent fellow. Made me wish I could do a little digging myself!'

'Did you hear anything about Raya Uma?' asked Jack, very much relieved that Bill had shown so little interest in their own doings that evening. He was determined to keep Bill on some safe subject now.

'Yes. The teacher knows him quite well, and likes him. Says he is a most interesting man and can talk on any subject under the sun! Even archaeology, which is rather a learned subject – the study of old buildings and other remains. He appears to think that Uma is here to study the old temples and so on that have already been excavated – but he's not, of course. That's just a cover for something *else* he's doing!'

Jack suddenly sniffed hard. A most delicious smell was coming from Tala's quarters. Fried fish!

'Yes,' said Mrs Cunningham with a laugh. 'Tala has been fishing – and we're having his catch for supper. Doesn't it smell *good*!'

'My word, yes,' said Philip. 'We've been having so many cold meals that I didn't even guess that Tala could cook. I bet Oola is pleased – he'll enjoy a meal like that.'

'That reminds me – Tala was very angry because Oola slipped off this evening, after you had all gone,' said his mother. 'He came to me in quite a rage. But as Oola had apparently done all the work Tala had set him to do, I didn't take much notice. I suppose he went after you, didn't he?'

'Yes,' said Jack. 'He came to guard his lord! He's cracked about Philip. I simply can't understand it!' He looked at Philip and grinned.

'I can't understand it either,' said Dinah at once. 'I mean – I could understand him having an admiration for Jack, because of Kiki – but why Philip?'

The conversation was cut short by Oola and Tala bringing trays. The big dish of fried fish, garnished with some strange greenery, and surrounded by most succulent vegetables, was hailed with enormous enthusiasm, and Tala grinned in pleasure as he saw the smiling faces that greeted him.

Oola was a little subdued. He had been well scolded by Tala, who had threatened to tell Bill how he had left his work and run off.

But when Oola had related to Tala how the children had been lost in the darkness, and how he, Oola, had rescued them and brought them safely back, Tala said no more. He did not praise Oola, for secretly he was jealous of what the boy had done, but at least he ceased to scold him.

Oola was very much hoping that Tala would let him share in this delicious meal, and so he was most attentive and obedient. Tala could not hold his anger for long, and had already made up his mind to give the boy a big help-ing as soon as he could.

Everyone set to and ate heartily, even Mrs Cunningham, who usually had a very small appetite. 'Tala would make his fortune in a restaurant as a chef,' she remarked. 'What *is* this sauce? I've never tasted any-thing so delicious in my life.'

'Better not ask,' said Bill mischievously. 'It might be a score or so of some peculiar insects mashed up – or . . .'

Dinah gave a small moan, and spat out a mouthful of the sauce at once.

'Don't, Dinah!' said Mrs Cunningham. 'Do remember your manners. Bill, don't say things like that. You've rather spoilt the sauce for me too.'

'Sorry,' said Bill contritely. 'It was just a bit of fun. I do agree that this sauce is marvellous. Ah, here's Tala. Tala, this sauce is fine. What is it made of?'

Dinah put her hands over her ears at once. She felt sure that it was mashed-up insects, as Bill had said, or water-snails, or something equally horrible.

'Sir, it is milk and onion, and bark of a tree called in our language Mollia,' said Tala, pleased at the praise. 'Also some mashed-up – mashed-up – how you call it? – er . . .'

'Insects,' supplied Jack helpfully.

Tala looked hurt. 'Tala not use insects. Tala use – yes – it is mashed-up potato – a very, very little.'

Everyone roared. It seemed so ordinary after what Bill had been suggesting. Tala smiled. He liked to make people laugh, though he certainly had no idea what the present joke was.

'Take your hands from your ears, Dinah,' said Jack. 'It was only mashed-up POTATO – very, very little!'

Dinah took down her hands, very much relieved to be told that the sauce was so harmless. The dish was soon completely empty, and everyone felt much better.

Oola was sent with a dish of fresh fruit, bought by Tala at one of the villages that day. It was about all that anyone could manage after the very rich fish.

When the meal had been cleared away, Tala and Oola sat down to theirs. Oola was very happy. Here he was, with the most marvellous meal in front of him, and the evening's adventure to gloat over. He had guarded his boss, and brought him safely back to the boat!

He began to tell Tala about it all over again, but Tala had no wish to hear such an epic twice. He told Oola to take the dishes and scrape them over the side of the launch.

'Fish eat pieces, fish grow fat, Tala catch fish, we eat again,' he explained to Oola, who saw the point at once.

Oola went to scrape the dishes, and suddenly caught sight of another boat gliding up through the darkness, its prow set with a single light. He stared at it. Would it pass by without hailing their own boat?

It slid into the bank, and stopped by the jetty. Bill had heard the motor, and was already looking over the side.

A man jumped out of the motor-boat and walked to where the launch was tied. He called up loudly.

'Anyone there?'

'Yes. Who's that?' Bill shouted back.

'Someone to see you!' came an answering shout. 'Can I come aboard?'

'What's your name?' asked Bill.

'RAYA UMA!' came the answer, and everyone on board sat up at once. Goodness – Raya Uma!

15

Mr Raya Uma

Bill was enormously surprised. He was so nonplussed that he didn't say a word.

'Hey – can I come on board or not?' said the voice impatiently. 'I heard there was an English family on the river, and I thought I'd like a chat.'

Bill recovered himself. 'Yes – come on up,' he shouted back. 'You took me by surprise. I wasn't expecting to hear an English voice here, I must say!'

'Shall we go away, Bill?' said Jack, in a low voice. Bill shook his head.

'No. Better stay with me. I don't know if he guesses who I am or not. Anyway, it's better if he sees a whole family aboard. Here he is!'

Tala had gone to light the man up to the launch. Now he was bringing him to where Bill and the others sat under an awning draped with mosquito-netting, lighted by a big lantern. Everyone gazed at him in interest.

They saw a medium-sized man, dressed in ordinary

summer clothes – flannel trousers, shirt and thin pullover. He wore a white linen hat, and had a beard and thin little moustache. He wore dark glasses like Bill.

He smiled down and the children saw that he had very white teeth. He bowed to Mrs Cunningham, and, as Tala held back the mosquito-net, he put out his hand. She shook it, and then he shook hands with Bill. He nodded at the four children.

'Ah – you've got your family with you, I see!'

'Yes – the children all had flu very badly, and the doctor said they should go somewhere warm – abroad if possible – so we decided to come out here,' said Mrs Cunningham, politely. 'I must say it's doing them a great deal of good.'

'Ah – and what are the children's names?' asked Mr Uma, smiling down and showing a lot of teeth.

Philip answered for all of them. 'I'm Philip – that's Jack – Lucy-Ann – and Dinah.'

'And what is the parrot's name? What an unusual pet!' said Mr Uma.

'Her name's Kiki,' said Jack. 'Kiki, this is Mr Uma.'

'Wipe your feet, blow your nose, fetch the doctor,' said Kiki politely, spoiling the whole effect by giving a terrible screech at the end.

'Don't, Kiki,' said Mrs Cunningham. 'Not when we have visitors!'

'How did you hear of us?' asked Bill, offering Mr Uma a seat.

'Oh, news soon gets round, you know,' said Mr Uma. He gave Bill a straight look. 'I've no doubt you've heard *my* name too,' he said.

'Er – yes,' said Bill, frowning as if he were trying to remember where. 'Someone told me of a Mr Uma who was interested in films at Cine-Town.'

'Oh, that's only a side-show for me,' said Mr Uma, puffing at his cigarette. 'My great hobby is archaeology.' He looked at the four children and made what they considered to be a very feeble joke. 'That's the study of arks, you know!'

The children ha-ha-ed politely. How old did he think they were, making feeble jokes like that? Lucy-Ann tried to see if he had the snake-like scar on his arm, but his shirt-sleeves were long, and she couldn't.

'We went to see an old temple outside Ullabaid this afternoon,' said Jack. 'Very disappointing. All front and no back – like the one at Cine-Town.'

Mr Uma took this as a joke and laughed too much. 'Ah, yes,' he said. 'Well, of course, archaeology *is* disappointing. Like the story of old Brer Rabbit, you know – "he diggy-diggy-dig but no meat dar".'

'I suppose it's very, very expensive to do a lot of excavating for old towns and so on, isn't it?' asked Mrs Cunningham, seeing that the children did not appreciate Mr Uma very much.

'Yes, Ma'am! You can pay out thousands of pounds doing that!' said Mr Uma. 'I've given it up; it's too expensive. You don't make any money out of it, either – your only reward is the excitement of – er – uncovering ages-old civilizations. All the same, it's a wonderful hobby. I've decided to combine an interest in films with my hobby – make a bit of money in films, and spend it wandering about this old, old country, making maps and plans of the last excavations and so on. And what about *you*, Sir – are *you* interested in that kind of thing?'

'About as much as the average man,' said Bill, cautiously, knowing that he was being sounded out about his own mysterious work. 'But any new experience is of interest to me. I write articles, you know, and one of these days I'm going to write a book – plenty of interesting things to put into it!'

The children smiled quietly to themselves. Bill did write articles. That was true – but this was the first time they had heard of a book. Bill *could* write a marvellous book if he were allowed to! The things he had seen and done were quite unbelievable. They felt proud at having shared in so many of his adventures.

'Ah – a writer! A man of leisure,' said Mr Uma. 'It's only you writers and you painters that can afford to dispense with an office and go all over the world to look for material for your brush or your pen.'

The children began to feel bored. It was quite obvious now that Mr Uma did not know for certain who Bill was, nor whether he had come out merely for a holiday or on some other mission. He and Bill had been 'crossing swords' so to speak, testing each other out. They felt that Bill was winning. He had persuaded Mr Uma that he was a writer, they were sure of it.

'Where are you going to next?' asked Mr Uma. 'May I offer you any hospitality? I have a little shack farther down the river – I'm on my way there now, actually. I would be pleased to give you dinner – such as it is – if you and your wife would care to come?'

Bill considered this invitation quickly. Should he accept? It would look odd if he didn't. Well – he might conceivably find out a little more if he went to Uma's house. So he nodded and thanked him.

'Well, thank you, that's kind of you. We'll be pleased to come. When? Tomorrow?'

'Certainly,' said Mr Uma, and got up to go. 'Tomorrow night at seven o'clock, shall we say? Your man will know the landing jetty at Chaldo, I'm sure. I will be there to meet you and take you to my house.'

'Stay and have a drink,' said Bill. 'I'll call Tala.'

But Mr Uma would not stay. He bowed very politely, and raised the mosquito-net. Then he almost fell over somebody crouching on the floor just outside.

He kicked out and there was a yell.

'Now then – who's this? Get out of the way there, lying ready to trip me up!' roared Mr Uma, losing his temper suddenly and surprisingly. He kicked out again.

Philip was up in a trice, guessing it was Oola who had crept up as usual to be near him.

'Mr Uma – it's only the little boy who helps our man,' he said angrily, and at once felt Bill's hand pressing his shoulder warningly.

'Sorry, Mr Uma,' said Bill. 'I hope you haven't hurt your foot, kicking out like that.'

Mr Uma didn't quite know how to take that. He recovered himself immediately, said good night quite heartily and was led off by Tala with a lantern.

'Oola! It serves you right if people fall over you, if you hide in corners like that!' said Bill.

'Bad man that,' said Oola. 'Bad, bad man. Oola come to guard boss from bad man.'

'Don't be silly,' said Bill. 'You don't know anything about him. Or do you?'

Oola shook his head. 'Oola know he bad man, Oola say so. Oola not seen bad man before.'

'Go behind with Tala,' said Bill. 'And don't come over to us again till we call you. Understand?'

Oola disappeared, and Bill went under the mosquito-net to the others. Uma's motor-boat had now been started up, and had gone down the river, disturbing all the stars reflected in the water.

'Well?' said Bill to his wife. 'What do you think of our friend Uma?'

'I don't trust him a scrap,' said Mrs Cunningham. 'He's, he's . . .'

'Slimy,' said Dinah, and everyone nodded. It was just the right word.

'What do you suppose he *is* up to?' said Bill. 'Anything?'

Mrs Cunningham considered. 'No,' she said. 'I think he's got a bad reputation and knows it, and he's nervous in case anyone *should* think he's up to anything and spy on him. I think he's probably hard-up, and making a bit of money in Cine-Town somewhere. He was so insistent on his love for old buildings that I feel his *real* interest must be in something else.'

'You mean he may be using this archaeology hobby of his to camouflage the business he's doing in Cine-Town?' asked Bill.

'Yes,' said Mrs Cunningham.

'Well, I bet whatever he's doing in Cine-Town is something underhand,' said Jack. 'Probably backing a shady little fair or something – or a string of shops – and having an interest in the film too. Plenty of irons in the fire.'

'Well, if that's the kind of thing he's doing, it's pretty harmless from my point of view,' said Bill. 'I am after bigger stuff than that – the kind of things I told you he had done before! If it's no more than messing about in Cine-Town, well, he's of no interest to the High-Ups!'

'Good,' said Mrs Cunningham, heaving a sigh of relief. 'I don't want you mixed up in anything dangerous, Bill – and I somehow think that Raya Uma could be very dangerous and very ruthless.'

'You're quite right, my dear!' said Bill. 'Now, what

about bed? I'll just go and stand by the rail. The stars are out beautifully now, and I shall enjoy a quiet ten minutes looking down the river.'

They all said good night. They were tired, and fell asleep immediately their heads were on the pillows. Bill stood silently gazing out, thinking of the strange Mr Uma. Then he saw a small figure creeping over the deck and settling down at the foot of Philip's mattress. Oola had come to guard his boss!

Oola sat up in fright when Bill came over, on his way to his own mattress.

'You may stay, Oola,' said Bill softly, and Oola sank down again happily. His lord was asleep – and he, Oola, was guarding him!

16

Next day

Next day Tala took the boat farther on down the river. They went very slowly, for Chaldo was only half a day's run, and they did not want to get there too soon. They passed some desolate country on the way, almost desert-like.

'Some of Mr Uma's beloved excavations must have been going on here!' said Jack. 'Bill, it certainly must cost an awful lot of money to dig over this enormous expanse – look!'

'It does,' said Bill. 'But there are rewards, you know. It's not only old ruined cities that are found lying beneath the mud and dust of centuries, it's treasure too.'

'Treasure!' said Philip, surprised. 'What treasure?'

'Well, much of this country held age-old buildings that housed the tombs of rich kings,' said Bill. 'Don't ask me their names, I've forgotten them.'

'Nebuchadnezzar?' suggested Lucy-Ann.

Bill laughed. 'You certainly know your Bible, Lucy-

Ann. Yes – probably even Nebuchadnezzar might have lived in a palace not many miles from here, or the great King Sargon! I really don't know. Anyway, when they died, they were buried in magnificent tombs, surrounded by their jewels and their other treasures, such as jewelled shields, wonderful swords, and so on.'

'My word!' said Jack, thrilled. 'And do you mean to say that things like that have been dug up – things thousands of years old?'

'Oh yes,' said Bill. 'They are in museums all over the world – bought gladly because of their historic value. They are valuable in themselves too, of course. I have seen one beautifully carved gold bowl, with bulls all the way round it, that must have been worth thousands of pounds. It was set with wonderful precious stones.'

'Well, then,' said Jack, 'I'm not so sure that Mr Uma's hobby isn't just the right one for him. Picking up priceless treasures for nothing!'

'That's where you're wrong,' said Bill. 'They can't be picked up for nothing – as I told you, a digging outfit, composed perhaps of fifty or so workmen, and a good sprinkling of white experts, may cost thousands of pounds. And we should certainly know if Mr Uma had an outfit like that!'

'Yes – I suppose you would,' said Jack. 'I mean – you can't *help* seeing wholesale excavations going on, can you? It would be in the papers too, of course.'

'Look – there are some ruins, over there!' cried

Lucy-Ann, pointing to the opposite bank. 'They look fairly recent. Would Tala know about them, do you think?'

'Go and ask him, if you like,' said Bill. 'I don't expect he can tell you much.'

The children went off to ask Tala. He nodded his head. 'Tala know. Tala's father, he dig there. Dig for treasure, much, much treasure. But no find any. All gone.'

That seemed to be all Tala knew. The children went back to Bill and repeated what Tala had told them. He nodded.

'Yes – he meant that whatever expert was in charge of the digging probably had a plan showing that royal tombs were to be found at a certain depth below – tombs possibly with much treasure. But when they got down to them, the graves were probably already despoiled and robbed.'

'But who did *that*?' said Lucy-Ann.

'Maybe robbers three or four thousand years ago,' said Bill, and smiled at Lucy-Ann's surprised face. 'I told you that this is an old, old land, that goes back thousands of years. Under the dust archaeologists may find ruins of city upon city, one built above the other.'

This was almost impossible for Lucy-Ann to grasp – city upon city! She tried to send her mind back through the centuries and to imagine the years passing over the land on which she was now gazing – cities rising, falling into ruin, other cities rising on the ruins and themselves falling into dust, only to have yet more towns built upon them.

She gave a little shiver. 'I don't much like thinking about it,' she said. 'Let's talk about something else, Bill.'

Bill gave her a hug. 'Well – what about lime-juice?' he said. 'Shall we talk about that, Lucy-Ann? It seems a very suitable subject for this hot day.'

'Oh, Bill – what you mean is that you want me to *fetch* you some,' said Lucy-Ann, who knew Bill's little ways very well. 'Jack – Philip – do you want some lime-juice?'

'Juice!' echoed Kiki. 'Juicy, juicy, juicy! Juicy Lucy! Send for the juice! Blow the juice!'

Philip was giving his snake an airing, and it was slithering round and about his feet. Lucy-Ann did not mind it, but Dinah did, so the boys usually chose a moment when Dinah was down below, doing something there.

'Isn't it a lovely creature?' said Philip, admiring the bright green of its skin, and the brilliant markings, or 'spottings' as the hotel manager had called them. 'It's a shame it's had its poison-ducts cut, isn't it, Jack?'

'Well, personally, at the moment, I'm glad it can't give me a poisonous bite,' said Jack.

The lime-juice arrived, Oola carrying the tray proudly. He was pleased to see the snake gliding round – his present to his lord! Dinah stopped dead when she saw it, and Philip picked it up at once.

The day went pleasantly enough, especially as, for the

first time, they came to a little cove where the water was clean and clear enough to bathe.

'You come in too, Oola,' said Jack. 'Do you good!'

But nothing would persuade the small boy to get into the tepid water. He touched it with his toe, yelped loudly and drew it back as if something had bitten him. He gazed in wonder and admiration as all four children swam and dived and kicked about underwater. He had been deputed to hold the bargua while Philip bathed, and he was very proud to hang it round his neck and keep it there.

Kiki was not very pleased with the way in which everyone deserted her for the pool. She flew to an overhanging branch and screamed at them.

Philip splashed her. 'Stop that row, Kiki! You sound as if you're being killed!'

Kiki flew high in the air, angry at being splashed. She flew down to the deck and waddled up to Oola for sympathy. But when she saw the snake hanging round his neck she backed away, hissing exactly like a snake herself. Mrs Cunningham smiled to see her, and made her come to her shoulder.

'Poor Polly,' said Kiki, into her ear. 'Poor, poor Polly. Jolly Polly, jolly Polly.'

'Well, which are you, poor or jolly?' said Mrs Cunningham, laughing. 'Now don't sulk, the others will soon be out of the water!'

'I wish we hadn't got to go out to dinner tonight,' said

Bill, a little later. 'It's a nuisance, Allie. I wish I hadn't said we would. I do so enjoy the quiet evenings on the boat.'

'So do I,' said his wife. 'Never mind – we don't need to stay long – and we *might* learn something; you never know!'

The boat glided on down to Chaldo and arrived about half-past six. Bill and his wife got ready and waited for Mr Uma to fetch them. 'You children have your supper,' said Mrs Cunningham, 'and then read and go to bed as usual. We shan't be late. Tala will look after you.'

'Here comes Mr Uma,' said Jack, spotting someone coming along in the dark, with a lantern. 'Goodbye – and keep your eyes and ears open! Mr Uma may not be as innocent as he seems.'

Mr Uma called up to the launch.

'Good evening! If you are ready I will guide you to my house. It is not very far. I am wondering if the four children would like to watch a dance in the next little village. There has been a wedding there, and the dancing is amusing to watch. My man here can take them.'

'Oh yes – do let us!' cried Lucy-Ann, and the others joined in.

'No, I don't think I want them to go,' said Bill firmly. 'I'd rather they stayed on the boat.'

'Oh, blow!' said Jack. 'Be a sport, Bill. We'll be all right, and we won't do anything silly, I promise you.'

'I think not,' said Bill. 'I'd rather you didn't go. Village wedding dances are not always safe to watch – your presence might be resented!'

There was no more to be said, but the four children were very disappointed. They called a subdued goodbye, and watched the lantern held by Uma's servant bobbing away through the trees.

'I wish we could have gone,' said Dinah. 'What harm could we come to, with Uma's man beside us? Blow!'

'Oh, well – it's no good thinking about it,' said Jack. 'I wonder what's for supper?'

Tala produced a fine meal, and when they were in the middle of it, the children heard him talking to a man who had come to the side of the launch.

'Who is it, Tala?' called Philip at once.

'It is Jallie, Mr Uma's servant,' said Tala. 'He say Master send him tell you go watch dancing. He say he change mind, you go.'

'Oh, good, good, good!' cried Dinah, delighted, and the others exclaimed in pleasure too. They finished their supper hurriedly, and called out to Tala.

'Tell the man we're ready. We're just getting our cardigans. It's a bit chilly tonight.'

'Oola go too?' said a small voice. But Tala overheard and called him roughly.

'No! You have work to do. Mister Bill send word you not go. You stay with Tala.'

Oola was bitterly disappointed. He made up his mind

to do his work quickly and then go to meet the others. He would soon find out where that village was.

'Goodbye!' called Lucy-Ann to the disappointed boy. 'We won't be long. Look after the boat, Oola.'

Oola stood looking after them in the darkness. A curious dread had come over his heart. Something was going to happen – something bad, bad, bad! Oola knew!

17

Extraordinary happenings

It seemed quite a long way to the village. The children stumbled along, and suddenly, for no real reason, Jack felt uneasy.

'How far is the village now?' he asked Jallie, the man with the lantern.

'It quite near,' answered the man, in a surly tone.

Ten minutes later there was still no sign of the village, and Jack spoke to Philip in a whisper.

'Philip, I don't like this. I don't feel easy in my mind. Ask him about the village again.'

'What about this village?' demanded Philip, tapping the man on the arm.

'It quite near,' answered Jallie again.

Philip stopped. He too now had a very uneasy feeling. He began to wonder if the message about going to the village dance was genuine. Suppose it was a way to get them off the boat – so that Uma could send someone to search it? It wasn't really at all like Bill to change his mind about a thing – especially when he had been so determined that they were *not* to go.

'Come!' said the man, and held the lantern high to see why they had stopped.

'Lucy-Ann – pretend you feel ill – cry, and say you want to go back!' whispered Jack. Lucy-Ann obeyed at once.

'J-J-Jack!' she cried, pretending to weep. 'I don't feel w-w-well. Take me b-b-back! Oooooooh!'

'Ooooooooh!' said Kiki, in sympathy.

'Oh, poor Lucy-Ann!' said all the other three, and began to pat her on the back. 'Yes, you shall go back.'

Jack went to Jallie. 'My sister must go back to the boat,' he said. 'She isn't well, as you can see. We must return at once.'

'No,' said the man. 'Come.'

'Don't be silly!' said Jack angrily. 'You heard what I said. Lead us back.'

'No,' said the man. 'I have orders. Come.'

'Look here – what's all this?' said Philip, joining in. 'There's something queer here. I don't believe you're going to take us to any wedding dance! Anyway, *my* orders are that we go back. Understand?'

Jallie glared at them. It was obvious that he did not quite know what to do. He could not make four children come with him by main force. On the other hand he certainly did not mean to take them to the launch.

The children glared back, Lucy-Ann giving sobs that were now becoming real, for she felt frightened.

'You *will* take us back,' said Philip slowly. 'See – I have someone here who will *make* you take us back!'

He slipped his hand under his cardigan and shirt, and pulled gently at the snake coiled there, fast asleep. The gentle pressure awoke the sleepy creature and it wriggled in pleasure at feeling Philip's hand on it.

The boy slid out the snake, and the man saw it suddenly in the light of the lantern. He stared at it as if he could not believe his eyes.

'Bargua,' he gasped, backing away. 'Bargua!'

'Yes, bargua! My bargua! He does what I say,' said Philip. 'Shall I tell him to bite you?'

The man fell on his knees, trembling, as Philip held the writhing snake between his hands. He pointed it at Jallie, and the snake darted its forked tongue in and out.

'Sir, I take you back,' said the man, in a shaking voice. 'Mercy, sir. Put your snake away.'

'No,' said Philip. 'I hold him near you, see, like this!' And he thrust the snake nearer to the man, who at once fell over backwards in utter fear.

'I send my snake after you if you leave us and run,' went on Philip, quite determined that he and the others were not going to be left in an unknown place in the darkness of the night.

'Sir, I take you,' whimpered the man.

'Well, get up and go then,' said Philip, cradling the

snake against him. It ran its forked tongue caressingly over the boy's wrist. The man shuddered – and for the thousandth time Lucy-Ann admired Philip, and the way he could tame all creatures and make them love him.

The man picked up the lantern and set off, his legs trembling as he walked along, thinking of the snake behind him, that very poisonous snake. What manner of boy was this that could harbour deadly snakes in his bosom?

He went along, taking the same path as he had gone before, though the children could not know this for certain, and just hoped for the best. The two boys were extremely worried.

'If Uma sent this fellow to take us goodness knows where, with orders to leave us stranded somewhere, whatever is he doing to Bill and Mother?' thought Philip desperately.

On and on they went, and at last through the trees came the welcome glint of silver water – the river.

'The River of Adventure!' thought Jack suddenly. 'My word – it's living up to its name.'

Jallie pointed with a trembling hand to the river. 'I bring you back,' he said. 'I go now, please.'

'Yes. Go,' said Philip, and thankfully the man fled with his lantern, stumbling in haste.

Someone came from the trees and flung himself down by Philip. It was Oola!

He moaned as he laid his head against Philip's knees.

'Bad men come,' he said. 'Bad men. What I do, what I do?'

In alarm Philip jerked him to his feet. 'Oola! Tell me quick – what's happened?'

Oola pulled them through the trees to the jetty. He pointed through the starlit night, and the others looked in astonishment and fear.

The launch was gone!

'Oola – what's happened?' asked Philip, shaking him.

'Bad men come. Bad men put Big Mister Bill and Missus on launch. Bad men get Tala and tie him up, and throw him on ground. Bad men take launch away, away, down river!' said Oola, sounding as if he were going to burst into tears.

'Whew!' said Jack, and flopped down on the grass, quite knocked out by all this news. The rest sat down too.

'How do you know all this, Oola?' said Jack, at last. 'Why didn't they tie you up too?'

'Oola just going after his boss,' said Oola. 'Oola creep away from boat – and then see bad men. Bad men no see Oola. Oola watch. Oola hide.'

'Well, we've now got a pretty good picture of what has happened,' said Philip grimly. 'Uma suspected old Bill of knowing too much – and so he's captured him very neatly. But what a pity Mother had to be captured too! *We* were going to be neatly put out of the way as well. Thank goodness for Oola!'

'And Tala,' said Jack. 'Tala's about too, apparently – all

tied up. We must get him. What in the world are we going to do?'

They got up and walked down to the edge of the water. Oola pointed to a dark shadow close by the bank, away from the jetty.

'Bad man's boat,' he said. 'Why he no take that?'

'I suppose because he wanted to hide away all evidence of us and *our* boat,' said Jack. 'I wish he *had* taken his own boat. Hallo – that sounds like Tala.'

Groans could now be heard somewhere nearby. Oola disappeared and then they heard him calling.

'Tala here!'

They all hurried over to him and there was Tala, so securely tied up that it was very difficult to free him! He was in two different states of mind at once – he felt extremely sorry for himself, and also extremely angry. He wriggled impatiently as the boys tried to untie him. In the end they cut the ropes and he rolled free.

Tala poured out his version of the happenings, pausing to bang his chest in anguish when he related how he saw Big Mister Bill and Little Missus being dragged away, and then yelled out in anger at the idea of him, Tala, being bound and thrown out like a sack of rubbish.

'Tala, listen,' said Philip. 'Was it Uma who came?'

'No. Other men,' said Tala. 'Servants. Bad men. Tala spit on them!'

'Where have they taken Big Mister Bill and Missus?' asked Jack.

'Down river,' said Tala, pointing. 'I hear them say Wooti. Tala not know Wooti. Tala very angry!'

'What *are* we going to do?' said Dinah. 'We can't spend the night out here – but where can we go? We don't know the way to anywhere.'

'Oola know,' said Oola's eager voice. 'Oola show you,' and he pulled at Philip's sleeve.

He took the boy away from the jetty, to the corner where Uma's motor-boat was tied. 'See – bad man's boat. We take, yes?'

'Oola! What a brainwave!' said Philip, delighted. 'Of course! Tit for tat. We'll go off in it now, straight away – back up the river!'

'No – let's go down to Wooti,' said Jack. 'It's probably just as near as the last village we visited. Let's hope it's a big place and we can get word about this to someone in authority. We can get news of our own launch there too.'

'Yes – that's the best idea, I think,' said Philip. 'Tala, can you manage this motor-boat?'

'Yes, yes, Tala know,' said Tala eagerly. 'We chase bad men, yes?'

'I don't quite know *what's* going to happen!' said Jack. 'But we're certainly not going to stay here and let Uma catch us in the morning! Come on – in we all get!'

And one by one they clambered into the motor-boat, while Tala tinkered with the engine. Now where were they off to? Wooti? And what would happen there?

18

Away through the night

They were all in the motor-boat very quickly indeed, half afraid that someone might come out of the shadows to stop them. Jallie might have gone to tell his friends that after all he had been compelled to bring back the children, instead of abandoning them far off in the darkness – and three or four of Uma's men might have come to look for them, and taken them captive.

But nobody came. Nothing stirred except the murmuring river, and the only other noises were the little sounds made by Tala as he tried to start up the engine. Oola patiently held a torch for him to see by.

'Click-click! Click-click!' The engine was coming to life – good! There – it was going!

'Buck up, Tala!' whispered Philip urgently, for the noise now sounded very loud in the stillness of the night. 'We may get some unpleasant callers if we don't go off soon.'

With a sudden roar the boat went off into midstream,

and the children heaved sighs of relief. It steadied, and then, keeping in the starlit centre of the river, it headed downstream.

There were no angry shouts behind them. Nobody seemed to know that they had gone in Uma's own motor-boat. Jack spoke to Tala.

'You said you didn't know Wooti. Do you know how far down the river it is?'

'Yes, Tala hear about Wooti,' said Tala. 'It is far down. Oola know Wooti?'

Oola didn't, but he remembered that another village was near to Wooti.

'Village name Hoa,' he said. 'We come to Hoa, Oola go there, ask about Wooti, yes?'

'Right,' said Jack. 'We don't particularly want to arrive at Wooti all set to be captured! We must tie up some-where some distance away, and then go in cautiously and see what we can learn.'

'Tala – will you keep going for an hour, say, then tie up somewhere so that we can sleep?' asked Philip. 'If we sail through the night we shall probably miss Wooti – we'd far better bed down for a few hours, as soon as we feel safely out of reach of Uma's men.'

'Well, as far as we know there were no more boats at Uma's place, so no one *could* chase us,' said Jack. 'Still, it's no good taking risks. Yes, drive the boat for an hour, Tala, and then we'll tie up somewhere.'

Tala steered on through the starlit night, and the

children talked quietly among themselves. Oola was contentedly sitting close to Philip, perfectly happy. Why should he worry? Were these children not clever enough to do anything, clever enough even to defeat bad man Uma? And anyway, he had the thrill of being near Philip all the time now, because the motor-boat was much smaller than the launch.

After about an hour Jack called to Tala. 'All right, Tala. We'll tie up somewhere. We don't seem to have passed any villages at all. This must be a deserted part of the river. Tie up anywhere.'

Tala's trained eye picked out a straight young tree on the edge of the left bank. He steered towards it, and it came to rest by the tree with a gentle bump. The engine stopped, and the quiet night closed in round them.

'Good, Tala,' said Jack. 'I'll help you to tie up. Then we'll all curl up and sleep.'

In five minutes' time everyone was fast asleep, though, like a dog on guard, Oola slept with one ear open! The two girls were huddled together, and the boys lay beside them, with Oola at Philip's feet. Tala slept by the wheel in a most uncomfortable attitude, snoring loudly at intervals. Kiki sat on Jack's leg and slept, head under wing.

They slept on and on. Dawn came and silvered the water. The sun rose and a pleasant warmth fell on the six sleepers. The bargua snake felt it, and slid silently out of Philip's shirt, to lie on his shoulder, basking in the sun.

Dinah awoke first, wondering why she felt so stiff. She

lay still, remembering the events of the night before. She moved a little to look round at the others – and she saw, quite close beside her, Philip's snake, lying on his shoulder, enjoying the sun.

She gave a scream before she could stop herself. Everyone awoke immediately, and Tala reached automatically for a knife he had somewhere about him. Oola leapt to his feet in front of Philip, ready to protect him to the death!

'Who screamed?' demanded Jack. 'What's up?'

'*I* screamed,' said Dinah penitently. 'I'm sorry – but the first thing I saw when I woke was Philip's snake looking at me. I just couldn't help it. I'm *so* sorry.'

'*So* sorry, *so* sorry!' chanted Kiki, and then gave a scream like Dinah's.

'Now don't *you* make a habit of screaming!' said Lucy-Ann. The snake had now slid into hiding somewhere about Philip, and Dinah felt better. They all rubbed their eyes and took a good look round.

There was nothing of much interest as far as the river was concerned. It ran on as smoothly as ever, lined on each side with trees that came down to the water's edge. What *was* of interest to the children was the motor-boat!

Was there any food or drink in it? Was it merely a boat that ran Uma here and there, as a car would run him about on roads?

'Let's see if there's any food,' said Philip, and they hunted round at once.

'Look at this!' said Jack, swinging open the door of a cupboard set under a seat in the bows.

They looked. It was full of tins! They read the names – there was tinned ham, bacon, sardines, fruit of many kinds and even soup.

'Funny!' said Philip. 'Why does Uma want to take food about in a motor-boat like this? He must have gone off sometimes on queer little jaunts, and stayed away long enough to need food – and yet not near enough to villages to get any.'

'Well, I don't care *why* he takes food about with him,' said Dinah. 'All I care is that he conveniently left some for *us*! And drink too – look, there are tins of lime-juice and orange-juice – they'll be very strong so we shall need water with those.'

Tala nodded his head towards a small enclosed tank. 'Water there,' he said.

But he was wrong. It was empty. So if the children wanted anything to drink it would have to be very strong undiluted orange- or lime-juice.

In another cupboard were ropes, powerful torches and big strong hooks. 'Whatever are these hooks for?' said Lucy-Ann, in surprise.

'They're grappling hooks – often used for climbing,' said Jack. 'Now why did Uma want those?'

'I know! For his hobby – archaeology,' said Dinah. 'Don't you remember? Well, if he goes about exploring all the old, deep-hidden places here, I suppose he *would* use these. Anything else of interest?'

'Some spades,' said Jack, 'and a small pick. Well, if Uma uses his hobby of studying old buildings as a camouflage for his other dirty work, whatever it is, I must say he seems to take it pretty seriously. Look – there are books about it here too.'

He pulled out books, some new, some old, all evidently well read, for there were small notes written here and there on certain pages.

'I'll have a snoop into these when I've had something to eat!' said Jack. 'I'm beginning to feel hungry now!'

So were the others. They found two tin-openers hanging on a nail in the cupboard. Jack promptly put one into his pocket for safety! They opened a tin of ham and two tins of pineapple, feeling that these might go quite well together. They drank the juice in the tins, but still felt rather thirsty.

'We ought to try and fill this water-tank,' said Philip, peering into it. 'It looks perfectly clean.'

'Tala and Oola fetch water next village,' proposed Tala. 'And bread.'

'Right. But we'll have to make sure it's not Wooti before we go boldly into it,' said Jack. 'Look at Kiki! That's her fifth bit of pineapple! Hey, Kiki, are you enjoying it?'

Kiki swallowed the last bit and flew over to the tin again. It was empty. She gave a squawk of disappointment. 'All gone!' she said, in a sing-song voice. 'All gone. Send for the doctor!'

'Fathead,' said Jack. 'Tala, are you ready to start? Stop at a village that you think is safe.'

Tala untied the boat and set the engine going. They chugged into midstream and set off. The sun was lovely and warm now, and everyone felt more cheerful – though nagging at their minds all the time was the worry of what had happened to Bill and his wife.

They came to a small village whose huts ran right down to the edge of the water. At once eager children ran to watch the boat. Tala swung in towards shore, where there was a small jetty for boats.

He conversed rapidly with a boy standing near. Then he turned to the others.

'He say this Hoa village. Wooti long way on. Two-three hours. He say will give Tala waterbag and bread. Yes?'

'Right,' said Jack. 'We'll come ashore and stretch our legs too. You and Oola go and see what the water's like. It must be drawn straight from the well. Draw it yourself, Tala. Come on, you others – it seems quite safe here, but all the same, we'll keep near the boat!'

19

The river is very peculiar

It was good to stretch their legs. Kiki as usual was on Jack's shoulder and created great interest among the excited children. They crowded round, pointing and chattering. Philip kept his snake hidden – he knew what a stampede it would cause if it so much as showed its head!

Tala and Oola had fortunately discovered a couple of large pails in the boat and had taken those to fetch the water. The children were glad – none of them liked the big skin bags, made of animal-hide, that water was so often carried in by the villagers.

Tala and Oola were a long time coming back, and the children began to feel worried.

'Why don't they come?' said Jack. 'I do hope nothing has happened to them. We *should* be in a fix without Tala.'

However, at last the two came, each carrying a heavy pail of water, and with loaves of bread strapped over their bare shoulders. Fortunately Tala knew enough of the ways of this family to know that they liked their bread wrapped and he had managed to get some cloths to wrap it in.

'You've been too long, Tala,' said Jack, not at all pleased.

'He talk and talk,' said Oola. 'Oola want to come back, but Tala talk.'

Tala glared at him, and then drew himself up to his full height. 'Yes, Tala talk. Tala find out much things. All peoples know Uma. He diggy-diggy-dig. Much, much dig. Peoples say Uma know where is big treasure. Much gold.'

Jack laughed. 'You've been gossiping. Uma likes to make people *think* he's digging for lost, long-ago things – but that's not what he's really doing. He's got something else up his sleeve – and I wish I knew what it was.'

Tala didn't understand this. 'What he got up sleeve?' he enquired. 'Big knife?'

'Come on,' said Philip impatiently. 'Let's put the water in the tank. I'd like a drink of orangeade straight away. I'm jolly thirsty.'

They all were. As the water splashed into the tank Jack considered it. It didn't really look very much for six people!

'Let's go on,' he said to Tala. 'We can look out for Wooti after two hours, if it's really two or three hours away.'

Tala started up the engine and on they went again. They passed quite a few small villages, and then came a larger one. Could this be Wooti? Jack glanced at his watch. No – they had only been going for an hour and a half, and Tala had been told that Wooti was two or three hours away.

'Tala stop?' called Tala. 'Tala ask name of village?'

'No. It can't be Wooti yet,' said Jack, and on they went. And then, quite suddenly, the river became very wide! The children were most astonished as the banks receded farther and farther away. It almost seemed as if the river had become a lake!

'Goodness! If the river gets much wider we shan't be able even to *see* the banks!' said Dinah.

Lucy-Ann stared out in amazement. 'Jack,' she said, 'we – we're not out at *sea*, are we?'

Everyone roared. Even Tala smiled. Lucy-Ann went red, and Jack clapped her on the back.

'Never mind! It certainly *looks* as if we're all at sea! I expect the river will narrow soon. Maybe the river bed is very shallow here, so the water has spread itself out well and made itself wide.'

Philip called to Tala.

'Tala! Better keep to one or other of the banks, or we'll lose our sense of direction. I can hardly see the right-hand one as it is!'

Tala swung over to the left to find the bank there. It was quite a long way away!

'I wish we had a map of the river here,' said Jack. 'Like the one Bill had, do you remember? It showed every village on it, and it would have shown us where Wooti came, and what happens to the river here – why it gets so wide, and if it narrows again!'

They were now close to the left bank instead of in midstream. The opposite bank could not be seen. The water seemed to stretch away interminably on their right, giving the impression that they were on the edge of the sea, sailing close to the shore – just as Lucy-Ann had imagined!

Tala was surprised, and a little afraid. 'The river's very wide here,' he said to Oola in his own language. 'We shan't see Wooti if it's on the other bank.'

This had also occurred to Philip. He pulled at Jack's sleeve. 'Jack – suppose Wooti is on the other bank? We'd miss it!'

'Gosh, yes,' said Jack. 'We can't even *see* the bank, let alone any village on it. Well – let's see – we'll get Tala to stop at the next little village on the left here, and ask about Wooti. If it *is* on the opposite bank we'll have to chug over there and look for it! Let's hope we haven't gone right past it!'

They looked out for the next little village, but the undergrowth was thick and grew right down to the water's edge, so that even if any village *had* been on the left-hand side, they could not have seen it. An hour passed, and the children grew uneasy.

'I *wish* we had a map!' said Jack. 'Blow Uma! Why didn't he keep maps on his boat! They would have been such a help. Hallo – I can see something on the right – yes, it's the right-hand bank come back into view at last!'

Sure enough a line of brown could be seen over to the right. It seemed rapidly to come nearer, which meant, of course, that the river was narrowing again, so that both its banks could be seen.

In fact, it narrowed so much that the banks were far nearer to one another than they had ever been before!

'This is extraordinary!' said Philip suddenly. 'The river flows in the direction we're going, as you know – we've been taking advantage of the current the whole time. Well – rivers usually keep either more or less the same width as they flow to the sea, or they get *wider* as other streams feed them by joining them. And they are at their widest as a rule when they flow into the sea.'

Jack stared at him. 'Yes. I know. Then – how is it this river has suddenly gone so small and narrow? Especially after being so wide! I know we're nowhere near the sea, and I can't imagine why it went so wide – just as I can't imagine now why it's gone so narrow!'

'It must have split into two streams – or perhaps more,' said Philip. 'Maybe it made itself into two separate rivers, some way back – one wide, one narrow – and we're in the narrow one. That's the only thing I can think of.'

'Tala! Stop the boat a minute,' commanded Jack. 'We must talk.'

Tala stopped the boat gladly. He was feeling extremely worried. What had happened to the river? Where was Wooti? What was the best thing to do?

They all talked together in the middle of the boat. It was a very serious conference and even Kiki did not dare to interrupt.

'Tala – what do you think has happened? Why has the river gone small? Do you think it split into two or three separate streams some way back?' asked Jack.

'Tala not know. Tala frighted,' said the man. 'Tala say, go back. This bad river now.'

'Well, *you're* not much help, Tala,' said Philip. 'We must have missed Wooti altogether. I bet it was on the right-hand bank – and we couldn't spot it because we were too far away. Blow! This looks like being serious.'

'Let's go on,' said Dinah. 'We're *bound* to come to some place soon, absolutely bound to.'

Jack looked over the side of the boat, to the left bank and then to the right.

'It all looks pretty desolate to me,' he said. 'Just a few trees only – and some mouldy-looking bushes – and then nothing but sand or dust in hillocks and mounds. Well – we'll go on for half an hour and then if nothing turns up – no village or anything where we can ask for advice, we'll go back – and cruise along the *right*-hand bank of the river. Maybe we'll find Wooti then.'

'Tala say, go back,' said Tala obstinately. 'This bad

river now. Deep, deep water, see!' He got up and pointed downwards over the side.

'You can't tell how deep it is,' said Jack, looking down into the water, which was now murky instead of clear.

'Tala know. Boat sound different on deep water,' said Tala confidently. 'Bad river now.'

'All right. We'll sail on bad river for another half-hour,' said Philip firmly. 'Then if there is no village anywhere we'll turn back. Start up the motor, Tala, please.'

But Tala stood there obstinately, and the boys' hearts sank. Surely Tala was not going to be difficult at this important moment? They could not give way to him. He would consider himself on top then, and any other decision they made might also be put aside by Tala.

'Tala! Do as you're told!' said Philip sternly, imitating Bill's voice exactly. Still Tala sat there, mutinous and obstinate.

And then, to everyone's astonishment, the motor of the boat suddenly started up, and the boat shook and quivered as it shot forward and sent everyone almost on their faces!

A voice came from behind them. 'Oola obey you! Oola drive boat for boss!'

With a fierce yell Tala leapt over to Oola. He rained blows on him and took the wheel from him at once. He shouted a long string of unintelligible words at the grinning Oola, and then, still with a very fierce expression on his face, he guided the boat down the narrow river.

Oola scrambled back, not seeming to have felt Tala's blows at all. He was smiling all over his face. 'Oola make Tala obey you!' he said, and was delighted at the grins he got.

'Jolly good, Oola,' said Philip. 'But don't do that kind of thing too often. You gave us all a frightful shock!'

20

Whatever happened?

Tala drove the boat rather fast, to show that he was still angry. Philip signalled to him.

'Slower, Tala!'

And Tala slowed down, afraid that Oola might come and show him how to drive more slowly. The boat went on between the banks, which were now narrowing even more. And then, as well as narrowing, the banks began to grow higher!

'Why – we seem to be going between cliffs now!' said Jack, in wonder. 'Tala! Don't go so fast!'

'Tala *not* go fast!' called back the man, looking puzzled. '*River* go fast – very fast! Take boat along. Tala stop motor, and you see!'

He stopped the motor, and the children did indeed see what he meant! The current was racing along at top speed, and the boat needed no motor to take it along – it was carried by the current!

The cliff-like banks rose even higher, and the children felt alarmed.

'We're in a kind of gorge now,' said Philip. 'A gorge that must be dropping down in level all the time, and making the water rush along. Hey, Tala, stop! This is getting dangerous.'

Tala called back at once. 'Tala no can stop! Boat must go on, on, on. River take boat all the time.'

'Whew! He's right!' said Jack. 'How *can* we stop? And if we did, where? There are only these high cliffs of rocks on each side now – nowhere to stop at all! We'll be dashed to pieces if Tala doesn't keep the boat straight.'

The children were very pale. Kiki was terrified and put her head under her wing. The boys looked up at the rocky cliffs on each side. Yes – they were now getting so high that they could see only a strip of sky. No wonder it seemed dim now, down here in the boat.

The water raced along, no longer smooth, but churned-up and frothy. 'It's pouring down a rocky channel, a channel that goes downwards all the time, and makes the water race along,' said Jack, raising his voice a little, for the water was now very loud.

'We must be going down into the depths of the earth,' said Philip, staring ahead. 'Jack – listen, what's that noise?'

They all listened, and Tala himself went pale.

'Water fall down, water fall down!' he called, above the roar of the river.

Jack clutched at Philip, panic-stricken. 'He's right. We're coming to a cataract! A gigantic underground waterfall! We're pretty well underground now, it's so dark. Gosh, Philip, the boat will swing over the top of the fall, and we'll be dashed to pieces. It sounds like an *enormous* cataract!'

The noise became louder and louder, and entirely filled the rocky gorge. It seemed to be the loudest noise in the world, and the girls pressed their hands to their ears, terrified.

Tala too was terrified, but he still had his hand on the wheel, trying to prevent the boat from crashing into the rocky sides. He suddenly gave a shout.

'We come to waterfalling!'

The children could not hear anything now but the roar of the waterfall ahead. Nor could they see anything, for the gorge was now too deep to admit much daylight. They could only clutch at the boat-seats and each other.

And then – and then – the boat swung violently to the left, almost turned over, rocked dangerously to and fro, and came to a shuddering stop!

All round was the sound of the giant cataract, but the noise had diminished. What had happened? Wonderingly the children raised their frightened faces and peered round. They were in darkness and could see nothing.

Philip felt something clutching his knees – a pair of hands. That must be Oola at his feet.

'Is boss safe?' said Oola's voice, sounding over the noise of waters.

'Quite safe, Oola,' said Philip, finding his voice trembling as he spoke. 'You all right, girls?'

'Yes,' they answered, but that was the only word they could manage to say. They were still clutching each other tightly.

'I'm safe too,' said Jack's voice, sounding unexpectedly cheerful. 'Hey, Tala! Are you all right?'

The sound of moaning reached the children, a doleful regular moan. Jack felt his way across the boat to Tala.

'Are you hurt?' he asked, feeling the man all over. He felt for his torch in his pocket and flicked it on. Tala was at the wheel, bent over it, with his hands over his head. He moaned all the time.

Jack could not see that he was hurt. He shook Tala, and at last the man looked up. He was shaking violently.

'ARE YOU HURT?' shouted Jack, thinking that Tala must have suddenly gone deaf.

Tala seemed to come to himself. He blinked at the torch and rubbed his eyes. He felt himself all over very carefully.

'Tala not hurt,' he announced. 'Tala good.'

Jack flashed his torch around to see where they were. They appeared to be in a quiet pool surrounded by walls of rock. How extraordinary! How did they get here, out of the raging torrent? Only just in time too, for the waterfall could not be far away.

He went back to the others, who were now recovering. 'Well, we seem to be safe for the moment,' said the cheerful Jack. 'I vote we have something to eat. Nothing like something in our tummies to make us feel better. Where's Kiki?'

'In that cupboard,' said Dinah. 'I heard a little unhappy squawk from there just now.'

Jack flashed his torch at the cupboard. The door was a little ajar, burst open by the tins that had rolled about violently. Kiki had gone there to hide in peace, away from the roar of waters.

'Kiki! You can come out now,' called Jack. And Kiki waddled out, her crest down, looking very old and bent and sorry for herself! She climbed all the way up Jack, as if her wings couldn't possibly fly, and was at last on his shoulder. She settled there, grumbling away, angry at all the disturbance she had been through.

'Get out a few tins, Dinah – you're nearest to the cupboard,' said Jack. 'Cheer up, Lucy-Ann. Philip, reach over to that lamp and light it, will you? It's the one used for the prow of the boat and ought to be bright. Buck up!'

It was a good thing that Jack took charge. He made everyone brighten up, even Tala, whose moaning still went on for a while. Soon they were all sitting together, munching sandwiches made of bread and ham, with orangeade to drink.

'Fun this, isn't it?' said the indomitable Jack, looking

round at the little company, lighted quite brightly by the boat's lamp.

Lucy-Ann managed a weak smile, though she felt that nothing could possibly be fun at the moment.

'Don't be silly,' said Philip. 'Let's enjoy our misery before we say it's fun! Gosh – I feel as if I'm in a peculiarly unpleasant dream. Anyone know what happened yet?'

Nobody did. It seemed an utter mystery. There they had been, whirling onwards to what must be an enormous cataract by the sound of it – and yet, all of a sudden, they had shot round to the left – into safety.

The food loosened their tongues, and soon they were talking much as usual. Tala condescended to take a sandwich, and he soon felt better too. He astonished the company by suddenly beaming round at them with the broadest smile on his face that the children had ever seen.

'What's up, Tala?' said Jack, amused. 'You look as if you've lost a penny and found a shilling!'

Tala looked puzzled. 'Tala not lost penny,' he said.

'All right, all right – forget it!' said Jack. 'What are you suddenly so happy about?'

'Tala brave man. Tala save everybody,' said Tala, beaming round again.

There was an astonished silence. Whatever did Tala mean? He sounded slightly mad, and certainly looked odd, sitting there in the light of the lamp, nodding his head up and down like a mandarin.

'I don't get it,' said Jack. '*How* did you save everybody?'

'Tala just now remember,' said Tala, still beaming. 'Boat go fast, fast, fast – big noise come – waterfalling near. Then Tala sees where cliff break – Tala swing boat round – bump-bump – boat nearly over. Now we here!'

There was another astonished silence. All the children stared at Tala, and even Kiki peered at him round Jack's face.

'But, Tala – you *couldn't* see a break in the cliff – it was too dark!' said Jack at last.

'Yes, yes,' said Oola's voice from beside Philip. '*Oola* see big hole too – big hole in cliff. Have good eyes for dark, Tala too.'

'Well, I'm blessed!' said Philip. 'I never saw a thing. But I suppose Tala must have been deliberately looking out for some break in the cliff, and caught sight of one just in time. He must have eyes like a cat!'

'Tala eyes good, very good,' agreed Tala, pleased at the interest he had caused. 'Tala see much, much. Tala save everybody. Tala good man.'

Tala looked as if he would burst with pride at being such a 'good man'. Jack reached over and patted him on the back.

'Tala, you're a marvel!' he said. 'Shake hands!'

This idea delighted Tala enormously. He shook hands very solemnly with everyone, including Oola – and was most gratified when Kiki too bent down and offered him her foot.

'God save the Queen,' said Kiki, in her most pompous voice, and gave a hollow cough, feeling sure this must be a solemn occasion.

'So *that's* what happened!' said Jack, handing round more sandwiches. 'Well, whether this is a dream or not – and I'm not really certain about it yet! – it's pretty exciting. Let's finish our meal and then do a spot of exploring. We may be out of the frying-pan and into the fire, of course!'

'Gosh – I hope not!' said Philip, looking round. 'But I can't say that I feel awfully hopeful!'

21

Much excitement

In about ten minutes' time they all felt cheerful enough
to want to get out of the boat and explore round the cavern they were in. It was not part of the gorge, that was
quite clear, for the rocky roof closed over their heads
about ten feet above them. The torches showed this
clearly.

'It's a big cave opening into the cliff from the gorge
outside that takes the river to the waterfall,' said Jack.
'That much is clear, anyway.'

'Tala see one, two, three others,' said Tala, nodding his
head. 'Boat go by fast. Tala no stop.'

'I see. Yes, I daresay there are quite a lot of caverns in
the sides of the gorge,' said Jack. 'The thing is – are they
just caves – or do they lead anywhere?'

'We'll have to find out,' said Philip. 'Now, before any
of us step out of this boat on to any ledge nearby, please
see that you each have your TORCH. We'll leave the
lamp burning on the boat – then we can all see it and

come back to it safely. But for goodness' sake keep together if possible.'

Tala had put the boat near to a ledge on the left-hand side of the cavern. He had managed to find a jutting rock nearby and had tied a rope round it. He was terrified that the boat might swing over the pool, and be drawn by the current into the river again.

Soon all six were out on the ledge. Tala had a powerful torch that he had found in the boat, and proudly flashed it all around. As far as they could see, the cavern stretched a good way back, ending in darkness.

'Perhaps this quiet pool runs right back, and becomes a kind of underground stream,' suggested Jack hopefully.

'What a hope!' said Philip. 'Why, we can't even see a way out for ourselves, let alone the boat. You're too cheerful, Jack. Pipe down a bit, or you'll be raising false hopes all the time!'

'Let him say what he likes,' said Lucy-Ann, flashing her own torch round. 'I feel as if I want to hear all the cheerfulness possible in this horrible place!'

Oola was well in front of everyone, scrambling about with a torch that was very faint indeed. But he seemed quite literally to be able to see in the dark! Jack called out to him.

'You be careful, Oola! You'll fall into the water and you know you can't swim.'

'Boss pull Oola out,' called back Oola cheerfully. 'Brave boss save Oola.'

That made everyone laugh. They scrambled about, flashing their torches here and there, getting farther and farther towards the back of the cavern.

The water ran back in a wide channel, a rocky ledge beside it on each side. The cavern narrowed at the end. Oola, who was first, shouted back.

'Ai! Ai! Here is tunnel!'

At once everyone felt excited. A tunnel? Then surely it must lead somewhere.

They clambered over beside Oola. He was right. In the centre of the back of the cavern the water stretched away into a narrow tunnel, pitch black and most mysterious!

'Could we get the boat along here, Tala?' asked Philip, excited.

Tala shook his head. 'Much dangerous,' he said. 'Boat get stuck? Water stop? Boat get hole? No, no. We go on. We see more.'

'Oh well – come on then,' said Philip, who had had wonderful visions of taking the boat along this underground tunnel and coming out into daylight somewhere else. He knew Tala was right, of course. They must explore much farther before they could plan to move the boat.

The tunnel ran on and on, curving at times to right or left. It sometimes widened, sometimes narrowed. At times the roof grew so high that it could not be seen; at others it came down low, so that it seemed only an inch or two above their heads.

'We could bring the boat along as far as here, anyway,' said Jack to Philip. 'Hallo – what's the matter with Oola? He's away in front there, yelling like anything!'

Oola was shouting in excitement. 'Come! Come see, boss!'

Jack and Philip made what haste they could, though it was not easy in this rocky, slippery tunnel, with the dark water waiting beside them.

They found Oola in a great state of excitement. He was peering through an uneven hole in the side of the tunnel wall.

'What's up?' asked Philip, pushing him aside.

'Bricks,' said Oola. 'Old bricks!'

Philip pushed his torch through the hole and gazed at something that was certainly a very peculiar thing to see just there!

His torch lighted up what seemed like part of a brick wall! But surely that could not be so? Who would build with bricks under the earth like this – and why?

'It looks as if someone built them on the other side of this hole to hide it,' said Philip.

'Or perhaps it's part of a *wall* built along some passage underground!' said Jack. 'Maybe the wall went past this hole – and wasn't meant specially to hide it.'

'Yes – but why should a wall be built *here*?' said Philip.

'It's most peculiar. Tala, come here – what do you make of this?'

Tala came thrusting forward. He shone his very powerful torch through the hole and on to the bricks. 'Ha!' he said. 'Old bricks. Very, very old. Tala see bricks like this before. Tala's father dig them deep, deep down.'

'Whew!' said Jack, startled. 'It looks as if this, then, might be a place where people long, long ago built tombs for their kings or queens. They were big places, weren't they? – deep underground – with passages leading to them.'

'We'd better read a few pages of those books of Mr Uma's, in the boat,' said Philip. 'Let's go back and see if we can't find out something about this place – surely that great waterfall must be marked, for instance.'

Tala squeezed into the hole, and struck the nearby bricks hard with the flat of his hand. To the boys' utter amazement they collapsed into dust!

'Tala clever! Tala see father do same, Tala remember!' said Tala triumphantly. 'Ai, Ai! *Now* what you do, Oola, son of a monkey!'

Oola had pushed Tala roughly aside and had squeezed past him, taking Tala's breath away. He leapt through the broken wall and stood beyond, flashing Tala's powerful torch.

'Here, here! A road is here!' he called, in excitement. 'Oola go!'

'Come back, you idiot!' yelled Philip. 'Don't get separated from us. OOLA, come back!'

Oola had already disappeared, but came back at once. 'Oola here, boss,' he said, in a subdued voice. Philip looked at him sternly, and then he and Jack also got through the hole in the wall, followed by the others.

Yes. Oola was right. Here was an underground way. Was it a passage made down to some old tombs? Had anyone else found it? Perhaps it was an underground cellar to some temple – or palace?

'Come on – let's go down it,' said Jack. 'This is too exciting for words. Keep together, everyone. Kiki, stop dancing about on my shoulder. Your feathers tickle. Keep still!'

'Keep still!' repeated Kiki at the top of her voice. 'KEEP STILL!'

Then everyone suddenly stopped in fright. An enormous giant-like voice echoed all round them. 'Keepstillkeepstill- KEEPSTILLKEEPSTILL.'

Lucy-Ann clutched at Dinah and made her still more scared. Jack was startled at first and then laughed – and immediately his laugh ran round and round, and came back to him, eerie and scornful. 'Ha-ha-ha-ha-ha-ha . . .'

'Oh dear – it's only an echo,' said Jack, lowering his voice so that the echo could not so easily catch it. 'It made me jump out of my skin. It's shut Kiki up all right!'

But at that moment Kiki lifted her head and let out one of her cackles of laughter – and immediately everyone

closed their ears in horror. The echo came at once, sounding like a hundred jeering giants laughing together.

'For goodness' sake, Kiki!' said Lucy-Ann. 'Don't do
that any more!'

'Come on,' said Jack. 'Are we all here? Where's Oola?'

But Oola had gone. There was no sign of him.

'Blow him!' said Jack. 'Where is he? We simply *must*
keep together!'

'Together!' shouted the echo. 'Together!'

'Oh, shut up,' said Jack, angrily, and back came the
echo. 'Shutupshutupshutup.'

Oola came into sight behind a rock. He was terribly
scared of the echo, for he had never in his life heard one
before. 'Come on, Oola,' said Philip, not unkindly. 'Keep
close to me. I won't let the echo eat you!'

They made their way down the sloping passage. It was
quite empty. The walls were of brick, and here and there
an archway of brick had also been made.

'Mud bricks,' said Jack. 'Not quite the same shape as
ours – more the shape of long loaves of bread with
rounded tops. Hallo – here's a big door. Can we get
through? I expect it is locked.'

Thousands of years ago it had not only been locked
but sealed too, for the old seal still hung there, waiting to
fall into dust. Jack pushed the great carved door gently –
and to his horror it fell into fragments, giving a little sigh
as it went. It was absolutely rotten!

What was beyond? Philip flashed his torch and saw

only a blank wall of rock. Then the light picked out something else – a flight of steps going down into the earth – down, down, down!

By this time the little company was so excited that nothing could stop them continuing their way underground! 'Come on – let's go down!' said Philip, and put his foot on the first step. 'Everybody here? Follow carefully – it's jolly steep. Talk about an adventure – this is the best one we've ever had!'

22

The mystery is solved

Before Philip could go down to the second step, someone pushed roughly past him, almost making him fall. Oola's voice cried out loudly.

'No, boss, no. Danger here, boss. Oola go first, boss. Oola go first!'

And Oola began to climb down before Philip could even grab at him. 'Come back!' yelled Philip, really angry. 'You hear me, Oola? Come back! What do you think you're doing?'

'Ai! Ai!' came a doleful yell, and there was suddenly the sound of a series of thuds. 'Ai! Ai!'

'He's fallen,' said Jack, in alarm. 'Gosh, isn't he a little idiot! These steps may be as rotten as that gate! Now what are we to do?'

Tala called out. 'Tala go get rope. Rope in boat. Tala go now.'

There didn't seem anything else to be done about it. Philip yelled down to Oola.

'Are you hurt?'

'Oola not hurt. Bump-bump-bump! Oola climb up again, boss!'

'Don't try! You may fall even farther next time!' shouted Philip.

'Gosh – he certainly saved *you* from falling, Philip,' said Jack. 'You'd have gone down with a crash. We were idiots not to think of that.'

'Let's sit down while we wait for Tala,' said Dinah. 'Poor Kiki – you don't like all this, do you? You've lost your tongue!'

They talked as they waited for Tala. They were all quite determined to go on. For one thing, they had to find a way out, that was certain. Jack wanted to go back *up* the passage to see if it led to the open air far above them. But Philip firmly said *no*.

'That would be idiotic just now,' he said. 'We'd be properly separated then . . . Oola down there – Tala gone to the boat – and us exploring somewhere else. The main thing at the moment is not to lose touch with one another. Ah – is this Tala? Good old Tala, he deserves a medal!'

It was Tala, with a rope from the boat. He had also brought a grappling hook, which was very sensible of him.

'Rope coming down now, Oola!' shouted Philip. Tala forced the great hook into a jutting-out piece of rock. He tied the rope to it, and he and Philip let the thin, very strong rope run down the old steps. Oola, down below, felt it slithering against him, and caught the rope in his two hands. With Tala and Philip pulling, and his own efforts at climbing, he was soon at the top.

'Well, thanks for falling down instead of me,' said Philip, clapping him on the back. 'But don't do it again.'

'Oola guard boss,' was all that the small boy had to say. Philip turned and spoke to the others.

'Well, now that we've talked over everything, we are all agreed that the best thing to do is to go back to the boat and have a meal and a rest. What's the time? Half-past six – gosh, no, it's half-past eight! Would you believe it!'

'Half-past eight at *night*?' said Lucy-Ann, and she looked at her own watch to make sure. 'Yes, so it is. Well, when it's as dark as this all the time, it's difficult to know *what* the time is!'

'We'd better have a meal, and a night's *sleep*, not just a rest,' said Jack. 'We'll all feel fresh in the morning. Then what do we do, Philip?'

'We have a good breakfast – we study the books up there in the boat, in case we can find out anything about this place, and get some idea whereabouts we are,' said Philip. 'Then we tie ropes round our waists, we each make up a fat parcel of food and we start off.'

'Right, boss,' said Jack, and made everyone laugh.

'Anyone think of anything else?' asked Philip. Nobody did, so the little party started off back to the boat. Through the hole in the wall, back through the watery tunnel, and lo and behold, there was the boat, rocking very gently on the big pool just off the gorge.

They all had a meal, and Kiki ate so much that she began to hiccup.

'Hiccup! Pardon! Hiccup! Pardon! Go in the corner!'

'Yes, that's where you ought to go,' said Jack. 'Greedy bird. You ought to be ashamed of yourself!'

'Let's get those books now and have a look at them,' said Dinah, when they had finished their meal. 'I'm not a bit sleepy. I feel awfully excited, really. I just wish we could be sure that Mother and Bill are all right.'

'I don't think we need worry too much, seeing that Bill is there,' said Jack. 'He's come through tougher spots than this. I think Uma has put them both carefully in hiding somewhere while he finishes whatever hush-hush affair he's on – something away in Cine-town, I've no doubt.'

'Do you remember how he tried to pretend he was so interested in archaeology and old buildings and things like that?' said Dinah. 'He thought he would put Bill off the scent!'

'Well, pretence or not, he's got some jolly interesting books here,' said Philip, who now had them all out on the deck, in front of him. 'Here, take one each – and see if you can track down this River of Adventure in any map, if you can find one – it will be called River of *Abencha*, don't forget.'

Neither Tala nor Oola took up a book. They did not feel confident about reading scholarly books of that sort

– in fact, Oola could hardly read at all. They sat and lazed, feeling pleasantly full.

'Here's a map!' said Dinah suddenly. 'Oooh – a good one too. Look, it unfolds out of the inside cover of this big book. No wonder we didn't find it before!'

They all looked at it. Jack gave an exclamation. 'It shows the river – see – going all the way down the page. This is fine. "River of Abencha" – that's the one. Now, let's trace the villages we've called at.'

'Here's Ala-ou-iya,' said Lucy-Ann. 'It's such a pretty name, I think. And I like its meaning too – the Gateway of Kings!'

'Yes – and here's Ullabaid, where we went to see that temple, and the children were frightened by Philip's snake,' said Dinah, pointing.

'And Chaldo, see – where that horrible Mr Uma kidnapped Bill and Mother,' said Philip. 'And where we took his motor-boat. And here's Hoa, where we got the water and bread.'

They traced the river down the page, their fingers passing over the names of villages they did not know. They were looking for the village of Wooti, to which Uma had probably taken Bill and his wife.

'Here it is,' said Jack. 'We *did* pass it then – look, it's where the river begins to widen. We were in midstream then, and didn't see it. Blow! We went right by it. Now see how the river widens in the map!'

They were following the curving river line with great interest. Philip gave an exclamation.

'It *does* divide – look! I thought it did. See, it actually divides into three. One bit flows to the east, one goes on to the south – and the third one is only just a tiny line – that must be the one that narrows into the gorge we went into. Yes, it is.'

They all looked. The third leg of the river was called, quite simply, 'Teo gra', which, Tala explained, meant Deep Gorge, or Tunnel. It came to a very sudden end on the map. That seemed strange!

'Funny! Where does the gorge water go to eventually?' wondered Philip.

'Underground, I should think,' said Jack. 'After all, it was pretty well underground already when we shot off into this cavern. After the waterfall it might be *right* underground. My word – I'm glad we didn't go with it! We certainly should be right off the map too!'

'Well, we've solved the mystery of the dividing river,' said Philip, pleased. 'Now let's try and find out what underground cities or temples or tombs are near here. Are there any marked on this map?'

'There aren't,' said Jack. 'I tell you what – let's look up Ala-ou-iya, Gateway of Kings, in some of these books. They might tell us something about the district round this curious gorge.'

They looked up Ala-ou-iya. Most of the books said exactly the same thing, to the effect that this part of the country was very rich in buried palaces and temples, and that only part had been excavated.

'Listen to this,' said Jack suddenly, and began to quote. ' "It is known that in the land around the strange and mysterious Deep Gorge there was once a most magnificent temple, far exceeding in beauty any other temple of that day (about seven thousand years ago). Excavations have continually been made, as it is likely that some of the greatest finds in the history of archaeology will be found here, and treasures beyond price. The temple was erected in honour of a well-loved goddess, and to her were brought gifts from kings and noblemen for many, many generations. These were probably placed in the underground compartments of the temple, and securely sealed. Whether robbers have been at work during the thousands of years since history lost sight of the temple is not known." '

'I *say*!' said Philip and Dinah together. 'Is it true, do you think?'

'Well – this is a very serious, *solemn* sort of book,' said Jack. 'I expect it doesn't go in for fairy-tales – only for what is true, or what is *likely* to be true.'

'What about that queer passage we found – and those steps leading downwards, through that old door?' said Lucy-Ann, sounding quite out of breath with excitement. 'Could we – could we possibly have found the way to some sort of old temple or palace, do you think – with the dust of thousands of years burying its ruins?'

'It's *possible*,' said Jack. 'After all – the entrance we found is not the usual one! I don't expect anyone has ever gone into this cavern before – how could they? Nobody in their senses would ever go into the gorge in a boat. We wouldn't have, either, if we'd studied a map and seen it marked.'

'And another thing,' said Dinah. 'I bet this gorge wasn't as deep as it is now, all those centuries ago. It must have been quite shallow then – it takes hundreds of years to make a deep gorge, cut right down into rock, like this one. I expect that all those thousands of years ago the gorge was quite shallow – perhaps not a gorge at all – and therefore our cavern entrance wouldn't be almost above water, as it is now – it would be far away below it. Nobody could possibly get into it then.'

'Dinah's right,' said Philip. 'The river-bed would be higher than this cavern, in those far-off days. That means that *we* have found a way underground to any old ruined cities there are here, that nobody else has *ever* found!'

This was a very startling thought. They stared at one another, deeply excited. And then a loud noise made them jump. It was poor Tala, so tired that he was fast asleep and snoring, even in the midst of this truly exciting talk.

'We'd better try to go to sleep too,' said Jack, laughing. 'Do you know it's midnight now? Leave the ship's lamp on, Philip. You can turn it down to a glimmer – but I'm sure we'd all feel happier if we had a night-light tonight!'

It wasn't long before everyone was sound asleep, and the tiny glimmer of a light showed no movement at all in the boat, except when Philip's snake slid out of his shirt and went scouting round to find something to eat.

It found nothing at all and had to return to the warmth of Philip's shirt, still hungry. It settled down again – and after that there was nothing to be heard except quiet breathing – and the constant, menacing roar of the torrent outside the cavern.

23

An astounding sight

Dinah woke first and switched on her torch. A quarter to eight! Goodness! She awoke the others at once and they all sat up, yawning and stiff. Tala turned up the light in the ship's lamp. He glanced round to see that everyone was all right.

'Ai! Ai!' he cried. 'Oola is gone!'

'Gone! He can't have gone!' cried Philip – and, at that very moment, Oola came into the cavern from outside, dripping wet!

'Where have you been?' asked Philip sternly. 'You are wet. Did you fall into the water? You cannot swim!'

'No, boss. Oola not fall,' said the boy. 'Oola go to see waterfalling! Oola go to see wonderful thing.'

'Well, I'm blessed!' said Philip. 'You little scamp! You might have been killed! How did you go?'

'Oola show boss,' said the boy eagerly. 'Wonderful, wonderful! Boss come? Quite safe, boss!'

He ran along the ledge beside the water in the cavern,

and stood at the opening. He turned and beckoned, his face shining. 'Come, boss. Oola show you.'

'Well, we'll see what he means,' said Jack, feeling a sudden surge of excitement. What a thing to see – that waterfall pouring down from the gorge, hurling itself over, and disappearing underground!

Oola had his torch, for although it was day very little light penetrated down between the tall narrow cliffs. Tala unhitched the ship's lamp and took that along too, feeling the same excitement.

The roar of the waters increased tremendously as they came to the entrance. Outside was a broad rocky ledge, just above the level of the tumultuous water.

'Follow Oola!' cried the boy. 'Safe, quite safe! Go higher soon.'

The spray from the water about three feet below them soon soaked them through. The ledge went steadily higher and was certainly broad enough to be quite safe.

Soon it had risen to about twelve feet above the water, and now the daylight was much stronger. The children snapped off their torches, and put them into their pockets.

The roar became louder and louder and beat painfully on their ear-drums. Oola led them onwards and up, and then stopped dramatically.

'Here, boss!' he shouted, his voice quite unheard in the din of waters. 'River gone!'

The six gathered together on a little natural platform,

and gazed down. The floor of the gorge came to an abrupt end just below them, and dropped in a sheer cliff of rock hundreds of feet down. Over this edge poured the swirling, tumultuous water in a mass of foam and froth and spray. It plunged down, and down, and down – nobody could see where it ended, for it went into utter darkness.

Far down below, strange lights danced and played, like little specks of rainbow, brilliant and glowing. It was a strange and magnificent sight, and nobody spoke a word as they stood and looked.

The spray flew so high that it fell on the platform of rock on which they stood, drenching them time and again. But nobody even felt it. They were nothing but eyes and ears, revelling in what must surely be one of the most astounding sights in the world!

The gorge itself went on and on – but there was no water in it beyond this spot – all the great torrent of river fell into this enormous fathomless hole, disappearing endlessly into the heart of the earth. That was the end of the river that ran through Teo Gra, the Deep Gorge.

'Where does it go to?' wondered Lucy-Ann, more awed than she had ever been in her life.

'To think that our boat might have gone over this, if Tala hadn't seen the cavern!' thought Philip, and shivered to his very soul.

'How beautiful!' thought Dinah. 'Those broken

rainbows down there – I shall never forget them all my life long!'

'Unbelievable!' thought Jack. 'Absolutely unbelievable!'

Tala thought it was time to go back. How long would these children stare and stare? He, Tala, was hungry, and water did not make a meal. He pulled gently at Jack's sleeve.

Jack turned, startled. Tala put his mouth to Jack's ear. 'We go back? Yes?'

'I suppose so,' said Jack, though he could quite well have stayed there all day. He nudged Philip, and together they all made their way along the sloping ledge, back to the cavern.

They were silent for quite a while. 'I feel as if I'd been to church,' said Lucy-Ann, voicing what they were all feeling. 'It was so – awe-inspiring, wasn't it?'

Kiki had not liked the continual drenching spray, and had not seen anything of the waterfall at all. She had hidden herself under Jack's cardigan, afraid of the noise and afraid of the spray. Now she was very glad indeed to be back in the boat, with a tin of pineapple being opened in front of her very eyes!

Breakfast was an unexpectedly hilarious meal. Everyone laughed a great deal, and Oola surpassed himself by laughing so much at Kiki that he actually fell over the side of the boat. Fortunately he fell on to the rocky ledge beside it.

They packed up as much food as possible when they

had finished, and tied string round it, after wrapping it in old papers. Tala hung two tins of lime-juice round his neck, and Oola was also very well laden.

'Now then – everybody got their torches? Everybody got their parcel of food? Everybody quite sure they will keep in touch with the one in front?' said Jack.

'Yes,' answered everybody, Kiki too.

'Got the ropes round your waist, Tala?'

'Tala have rope,' said Tala. 'And hook. And Tala have trowel and fork!'

So he had, all tied with string somewhere about his person. He had wanted to take a spade too, but all the spades were heavy, and it didn't seem possible to drag one about all the time, strong though Tala was.

'You're carrying as much as a camel,' said Philip, with a laugh.

'Oola carry like camel too,' said Oola at once, jealous of any praise of Tala from his boss.

'Oh, Oola carry like *two* camels!' said Philip, and the plucky little boy was happy at once.

'Well, I suppose it's goodbye to this boat,' said Philip, looking round it. He stopped and picked up something.

'What's that?' asked Dinah.

'Oh, just an idea of mine,' said Philip. He tore a page or two out of one of Uma's books and stuffed them into his pocket.

'It's some pages that Uma marked,' he said. 'If he

thought them important enough to mark, we may as well take them. You never know – they might come in useful!'

They set off along the little ledge that ran alongside the water in the cavern. They came to the hole that had once been backed by the old brick wall, which Tala's hand had touched and crumbled into dust.

They went through it and stood in the passageway. It was dark all around them, save for their torches.

'We'd better just explore this passage upwards and make sure that we *can* get out that way, before we explore that exciting-looking flight of steps we found,' said Jack. 'I expect the passage leads to ground-level.'

'I sincerely hope so!' said Philip. 'Though I have my doubts. Surely if there were a way out up there, other people would have found it and come in by it? Yet that sealed door that fell into bits was still in place.'

'Yes – and that looks as if nobody *had* come down here since it was put there,' said Dinah. 'Well – let's go on up!'

They went upwards, shining their torches into the darkness – but some way up the passage they came to a full stop. A wall of stone greeted them, built right across the passage.

This wall was not made of mud bricks that crumbled at a touch! It was made of solid blocks of stone, set in rows, one above the other. Now it was plain why no one had ever come that way! At some time someone must have ordered the stone wall to be built, to block up completely the entrance to whatever was below.

'No good,' said Philip, a little cold feeling gripping his heart. 'No way out here. 'We'd better go downwards again – to that old flight of steps. *They* may lead us somewhere!'

24

A Strange and wonderful find

Jack looked at Philip in the light of the torches. Philip pursed up his lips and put on a grim look – they were certainly up against things now! He nodded his head towards the girls, warning Jack not to frighten them. Jack nodded back.

They went down the passage to where the rotten old gate had been. They came to the flight of steps. Although these were of stone, the edges had crumbled badly, which was why Oola had slipped and fallen. Even so, he had not fallen right to the bottom!

'Tala, you and Jack hold the end of the rope,' said Philip, who had now taken command. 'Send the other end down the steps – that's right. Now, I'll take hold of it and go down carefully, examining the steps, and counting them – and if I come to a rotten one I'll shout up what number it is, so that when we all go down we can be extra careful when we come to that step.'

'Good idea,' said Jack. He and Tala held the rope

firmly and Philip began to go down. Oola was prevented by Tala from pushing in front and going down first, or he would have done exactly the same as he had done before. He was very angry, but it was no good – he had to stay behind.

Philip went slowly and carefully down the steps, counting as he went. 'One, two, three, four – number four is crumbling, Jack – five, six, seven, eight, nine – number nine is almost gone – ten, eleven . . .'

'One, two, six, five, ten!' shouted Kiki, thinking this was a number game. 'One, two, good fat shoe, nine ten, buckle my hen, three four . . .'

'Number fifteen is gone – and number sixteen,' called Philip.

'Four, nine, fifteen, sixteen,' repeated Jack. 'Shout louder, Philip – it's difficult to hear you now you're going down.'

'Right,' yelled back Philip, holding tightly to the rope, afraid of missing his footing. 'These steps are jolly steep. You'll all have to be careful!' He went on calling up the numbers, but when he came to number thirty-nine they could hardly hear his voice. There had been so many missing or crumbling steps that Lucy-Ann had had to find a pencil in Jack's pocket and scribble them down in his notebook.

'I'm at the bottom now,' yelled Philip.

'WHAT?' yelled Jack.

'I'M – AT – THE – BOTTOM!' yelled back Philip. 'Let Dinah come next. BE CAREFUL!'

Dinah set off down the steps. The others heard her counting them, and when she came to a bad one they shouted a warning to her. But Dinah had them all in her memory. She managed very well indeed, holding hard on the rope. At last she was standing beside Philip.

Then came Lucy-Ann. She was more afraid than Dinah, and slipped at the fifteenth step. But her hold on the rope saved her, and she soon recovered her balance.

Then Jack came, steady and sure of foot. It seemed a very long way down. The steps were very steep at times, and the hole down which they went was not very wide.

'Now that's us four here,' said Philip, shining his torch. 'Tala, send Oola down!' he shouted.

But Tala came next instead. He explained that Oola wanted to come down last of all, and didn't need the rope. He had sent it slithering down the steps after Tala had reached the bottom.

'He'll fall and break his leg,' said Jack, vexed. 'He's a fathead!'

But even as he spoke Oola was beside them, grinning in the light of the torches. Now that he knew that so many steps were rotten, he had been careful. He was as surefooted as a cat in his bare feet.

'Oola here, boss,' he announced to Philip.

'Now – where do we go from here?' wondered Philip. He shone his torch in front of him. There was another passage there, narrower than the one above the steps. Its walls were made of the same kind of bricks they had seen before. The children did not dare to touch them in case they too fell into dust. There was something rather horrible about that!

They went along the passage, which sloped quite steeply downwards, and came to an archway, also built of bricks.

'I suppose they kept making these archways in order to strengthen the roof of the passages,' said Jack. 'It's amazing that some of them haven't fallen in.'

'I bet a lot of them have,' said Dinah. 'I hope nobody sneezes while we're down here – I feel as if it might bring the roof crashing in on top of us.'

'Don't,' said Lucy-Ann sharply. 'I'm afraid of that too.'

The passage led them to a kind of room, almost round, with a great door at the farther end. The children stopped and flashed their torches round. In one corner was a curious heap of many things, and they went over to them.

But even as they came near, the sound of their footsteps disturbed the air enough to make the little heap crumble into dust! With small sighs it settled into a much smaller heap – but one thing still stood, solid and bright.

'What is it?' said Dinah, not daring to touch it. Very carefully Jack picked it up. It shone brightly.

'A bowl!' he said. 'A golden bowl! Set with stones, look, all round the edge. Gold is one of the things that never perishes, or loses its colour – and this bowl has lasted all through the centuries! Isn't it lovely!'

They all looked at it in awe. How old was it? Three, four, five thousand years old? Who had used it? Who had carved these camels round it? It was beautiful!

'This must be priceless,' said Philip, in wonder. 'It must have contained offerings to some god or goddess that the people of those days worshipped. My word – this is wonderful!'

'Philip – do you think – is it *possible* that we're near the lost temple of that well-loved goddess you read about in Uma's book?' asked Lucy-Ann.

'I should think it's *quite* possible,' said Philip, running his hand round the bowl. 'We may even now be getting near to the temple itself – or perhaps we are under it – and coming to the compartments beneath it where gifts were stored! My word – no, surely such a thing couldn't really happen!'

'It might – it *might*!' said Dinah, excitement almost choking her voice.

Oola and Tala were most interested in the bowl, particularly Tala. 'Gold!' he said, tapping the bowl. 'Tala know gold. This gold!'

'Carry it, Tala,' said Philip, 'and don't dare to drop it! Now, what about this door? It is sealed.'

Oola ran to it, and shook the great seal. It dropped into his hands! Philip went to the door and pushed at it. It suddenly sagged on its hinges and then fell away from them, hanging oddly sideways, leaving a gap big enough for everyone to climb through.

And now it was quite obvious that they were in some old and mighty building! Here were great rooms, stretching one into the other, some with doors that had crumbled, some with no doors at all.

'They're rather like great cellars,' said Jack, as their torches shone down square compartments built of stone, and then on oblong ones, then on communicating passages. It was a vast labyrinth, and piled everywhere were strange heaps of unrecognizable things. Everything had perished except what was made of metal or stone.

'Look – here's a tiny statue, standing in a niche of its own,' said Lucy-Ann, and she picked it up. It was carved out of some curious stone – most beautifully done, with every fold of the robes lovingly wrought. They all looked at it. How old was it? How many, many centuries ago had some craftsman toiled over it in delight for weeks or months? Who had brought it to the temple to give to the goddess? They would never know!

They began to examine some of the things set in heaps. Gold always stood out well, for its colour was unchanged – and there was much gold! Gold statues, gold bowls, gold combs, gold ear-rings, gold ornaments . . .

In one small square room there were swords, their hilts set with precious stones. What stones? Nobody knew! Jack picked up a dagger whose hilt was carved and ornamented with gold. 'I'd like this!' he said.

'We can't take anything!' said Philip. 'Except what we need in order to show the value of our discovery.'

'Right. Then I'll take this dagger,' said Jack, and stuck it into his belt.

'I'll take this gold comb,' said Dinah. 'I'll wear it in my hair!'

'I'll have this tiny statue,' said Lucy-Ann. 'I wish it really *could* be mine – it's beautiful. But of course, these things can never belong to any one person – they belong to the whole world, because they are bits of real, long-ago history.'

'You've said exactly what I was thinking myself, Lucy-Ann,' said Philip. 'I'm taking along this cup – at least, I think it's a cup. It's gold – and look at the carvings of bulls all round it! Marvellous!'

They went on until at last they came to the end of the store-rooms. They felt quite bemused by the thousands of things they had seen! No robbers had been here, that was certain. Here were treasures that had been undisturbed through all the ages that had passed since they had been given to the goddess of the temple!

'Boss, Oola wants sun,' said Oola to Philip. 'Oola doesn't like dark. Doesn't like this place.'

'Well – I expect we all feel that we want a bit of sun,' said Philip. 'But has anyone seen a way upwards, a way out of these underground cellars? *I* haven't!'

25

Is there a way out?

They had all been so interested and absorbed in the treasure they had found that they had quite forgotten their
danger. Jack sat down on a stone seat. He sat down gin-
gerly, half afraid it might crumble as did so many things
in these store-rooms. But it was of stone, and bore his
weight safely.

'There must have been *some* way down to these store-
rooms,' he said. 'Two or three ways, I should have
thought, because they're so vast in extent. Anyone see any
steps downwards?'

'Only those we came in by,' said Philip. 'Maybe that
was the only entrance.'

'No. I should think that was a secret entrance, used by
the priests,' said Jack. 'There must have been some more
usual way into this place. I imagine that the temple itself
was immediately overhead — it must have been an enormous place!'

'Yes — but don't run away with the idea that it's there

still, rising magnificently into the air!' said Philip. 'It was in ruins thousands of years ago, and other buildings may have been set above it, and yet others above them! We may be far down under the earth – and probably are. You read bits of those books in Uma's boat, didn't you? We are in a long-ago, lost, forgotten place, which we have happened on by chance.'

Everyone listened to this in silence. Lucy-Ann gave a little shiver. Long-ago – lost – forgotten – they were somehow sad, frightening words. It was strange too, to think that above their heads might be ruins of several other temples, also lost and forgotten.

'I want to get out of here,' said Lucy-Ann suddenly. 'I feel frightened now.'

'Let's have something to eat,' said Jack at once. Everyone always felt better after a meal, he had noticed – including Lucy-Ann, whose imagination was more vivid and sensitive than that of the others!

So they sat down in one of the temple store-rooms and enlivened the centuries-old silence by chatter and even laughter, for Kiki decided to join in the meal and the chattering too.

'Where's your hanky?' she demanded of the surprised Tala. 'Blow your nose! One, two, how do you do? Wipe your feet, knock-knock, who's at the door? A-whooooo-shoo!'

Her sneeze was so realistic that Tala and Oola stared in wonder. Then Kiki practised various kinds of hiccups, and Tala gave one of his guffaws, which echoed round and round the little stone chamber in a most remarkable way, quite silencing Kiki. It also disturbed a small, mouldering heap of things in a nearby corner, and they subsided with one of the odd little sighs that the children now knew so well.

'There, Tala – see what your laugh has done,' said Jack, pointing. 'You'll have the whole place down on our heads if you laugh as loudly as that!'

Tala was quite horrified. He gazed at the roof by the light of his torch as if he really thought it might be coming down. Oola gazed too. He was very silent, and obviously scared and unhappy. He kept very near to Philip.

Tala threw down the wrapping from his sandwiches. 'No, don't do that, Tala!' said Jack at once. 'Please pick that up! It's a shame to litter up a place like this with modern newspapers!'

Tala picked up the paper, looking as if he thought that Jack was quite crazy. Philip felt about in his pocket, and pulled out the two or three pages he had torn out of one of Uma's books – the ones on which Uma had made notes.

'I'll just have a look at these,' he said. 'I don't expect they'll be of any help, but they might. I have an idea that this place we're in is the one that interests Uma – and, knowing what is here through seeing it with our own eyes, I am beginning to feel that we've made a big mistake about Uma.'

'How do you mean?' asked Jack. 'We were more or less certain that he was using his "hobby" of archaeology to cover up his real affairs in Cine-Town, weren't we? Do you mean that we were wrong?'

'Yes. I think his *real* business *is* archaeology!' said Philip. 'But not because he is interested in history or old buildings – oh no! All that Uma is interested in is getting at the priceless treasure that he thinks may be here! He's just a mean, ordinary robber – all his digging is merely to find and steal the kind of treasure we can see around us this very minute! He is after such things as that gold bowl we gave Tala to carry, and . . .'

'Yes! You're right!' cried Jack. 'And probably just as he is feeling that his excavating is almost at an end, and he'll soon be able to take what he wants, along comes Bill! And Uma's afraid, because he knows Bill's reputation, and is certain he's come out here to watch him!'

'That's it!' said Philip. 'And he makes his plans carefully – kidnaps Bill and Mother – plans to get *us* out of the way too – and to finish his digging and clear off with the spoils!'

'Whew!' said Dinah, quite overcome by all this explanation. 'I think you're right! And what happens is that we go off in Uma's boat, and actually find the treasure chambers ourselves!'

'Yes – but we're up against a very big snag,' said Philip soberly. 'We don't know how to get out of here!'

'Have a look at those notes of Uma's. See if there's any-

thing in them to help us,' said Lucy-Ann. 'He was looking for this place, wasn't he? – and you said that you
thought he had almost finished his excavations – so his
digging must have brought him very near these treasure
chambers! Look at his notes!'

Philip spread out the marked pages on the floor, and
Tala shone his powerful torch on them. The children
knelt down to examine them.

On one page was a list of the buildings that were
known to have been built over the site of the great temple. Uma had put ticks beside them, and also the word
'Trouvé'.

'Trouvé! That's French for found,' said Jack. 'That
means that in his digging he has come across some of
these other remains and has dug through them. Yes – he's
done well. He must be very near here in his digging. I
wonder how many men he's got on the job. It's usually a
very long job, isn't it, Philip?'

'Not if you're merely a *robber* and not an archaeologist!' said Philip. 'A man really interested in old things
would not dig straight through them, destroying all kinds
of interesting bits of history – he would go carefully, bit
by bit – sifting the soil, examining everything. But
Uma . . .'

'Yes – Uma's only a robber! All he'd do is to pay work-
ers to dig, and tell them where – and to dig fast!' said
Jack, interrupting. 'Gosh – he's clever!'

'Not clever,' said Dinah. 'Just smart! Horrible man!

191

Do you suppose his men are digging over our heads this very minute?'

'Maybe!' said Philip. 'Hallo, look – here's a little map he's drawn. Is that any use to us?'

They pored over it, but could not make out what it was meant to be. Philip sighed. 'Well – except that they give us an idea of Uma's real business, these papers aren't much help. Come on – let's *really* hunt for an exit. There simply must be some way out of these underground chambers into the temple that was above.'

They wandered all over the store-rooms again, becoming very tired of the darkness and the mustiness, which seemed to be more 'smellable' now, as Dinah kept pointing out. Oola was frankly miserable, and trailed along after Philip, dragging his bare feet dejectedly.

They sat down again at last in the biggest store-room of all. 'The only thing I can think of is to climb up those steps again, and go all the way back to the boat,' said Philip at last. 'I honestly don't see any sense in staying here any longer – there doesn't seem to be ANY way out!'

'What's the good of going back to the boat?' said Jack gloomily. 'There's no way of escape from that cavern!'

'I don't know about that,' said Philip. 'You remember that rocky platform that Oola took us to – where we looked down and saw the river disappearing far below? Well, there *might* be a chance of climbing up and up the sides of the cliff at the side of the gorge, and getting to the top.'

'Impossible!' said Jack. 'I had a jolly good look when we were there. Still – we'll go back and see. I agree that it's no good sitting here. Nobody's likely to rescue us!'

Most dispiritedly they made their way back through the vast range of store-chambers. They came to the door that still hung partly on its hinges, and climbed past it into the room where they had found the beautiful golden bowl, and then through that and into the narrow passage beyond, that led to the steep steps.

'Oola – go up first, you climb like a cat,' said Philip. 'Tala, give him the rope to take up, and the grappling hook. Oola, need help. You must run up the steps carefully – CAREFULLY – with rope and hook. Do you understand?'

Oola was a different being at once, now that he thought they were leaving the great rooms down below. He nodded eagerly and took the rope. Ah – he was doing something for his boss – something important. He, Oola, and not Tala! Very proudly he began to climb the steps, feeling each with his hands before he trod on it. He slipped once, but managed not to fall.

At last he was at the top, and yelled down.

'Oola here! Oola safe! Here comes rope!'

Oola let the rope slither down the steps, carefully holding the other end himself. He had tied it to the big hook, which he now stuck firmly into a jutting-out rock as he had seen Tala do before.

The rope tightened in his hands and he knew that

someone was climbing. Perhaps his boss? Oola held on tightly, bracing himself behind a rock, in case Philip slipped and had to pull on the rope to save himself.

And then Oola heard something that scared him almost to death! It was a knocking sound away up the passage behind him! Knock-knock – thud, thud, thud! Oola's heart turned over and he fell to the ground in fright, letting the rope go slack.

At once he heard Philip's voice. 'Tighten the rope, Oola – it's slack! Hey, what are you doing?'

Knock-knock-thud-thud! Was it the old gods and goddesses coming back, angry because people had been in their temple? Oola screamed loudly, and Philip almost fell down the steps in alarm.

'The gods! They come!' screamed Oola. 'They come!'

26

'The gods! They come!'

Philip couldn't hear what the boy was screaming and he was most alarmed. He hurriedly climbed the rest of the steps, trying to be extra careful, for Oola had forgotten all about holding the rope tight, he was so terrified.

'Oola! What's up? What are you screaming for?' demanded Philip, as soon as he had reached the top.

'The gods!' cried Oola, pointing up the passage. 'They come. Listen, boss!'

Philip had heard nothing but Oola's screaming when he was climbing the steps – but now to his startled ears came the sound of the knocking that Oola had heard!

Knock-knock-knock-knock! Thud!

Philip stared up the dark passage, his heart beating. For one wild moment Oola's terror infected him, and he imagined angry gods demanding entry. What *was* that noise?

He turned and called down. 'Come up, quickly! Something's happening!'

His hands trembling, he held the rope as tightly as he could, with Oola clinging to his knees, quite weak with fright. Dinah came up, alarmed at Philip's shout. As soon as she stood beside him she heard the knocking too and was very scared, especially as she heard Oola's continual plaintive moans.

'The gods! They come! They come!'

The others climbed up, Tala last. As soon as he heard the knocking he turned in fright to go down the steps again, missed his footing and rolled cursing to the bottom. He too thought that the gods had come to revenge themselves on the little company of people who had dared to wander through their temple rooms!

Philip had no time to think of the terrified Tala, nor even to wonder if he were hurt. He had to decide what to do about the knocking. Where exactly did it come from?

'It's somewhere up the passage – and we know there's no way in, because we've been there and seen the wall of stone that is built right across!' said Philip. 'Jack – do you think it is Uma and his men?'

'Can't be anyone else,' said Jack. 'Do shut up, Oola. I can't hear myself speak.'

Knock-knock-knock!

'They come, they come!' moaned Oola, still clinging to Philip's knees.

'Uma must have found a plan or map that somehow enabled him to dig down to this passage,' said Philip, thinking hard. 'But instead of coming in at *this* side of that stone wall, they dug down just behind it. They must be trying to break the wall down. What a hope!'

'They'll do it, though,' said Jack, listening. 'They've got some powerful tools. Quick, Philip, what's our plan?'

'Can't think of one. It's all so sudden!' groaned Philip. 'Gosh, I'm glad to know that at any rate we'll be able to get out of here!'

'Uma won't be pleased to see us, if it's really him and his men,' said Jack soberly. 'Well, we can't do anything but wait. Philip, I'm afraid Uma is going to rifle those temple store-chambers now – and take away things that are of absolutely priceless value. I don't see how we can prevent that.'

'I wish we could!' said Philip, and the girls echoed his wish. It was shocking to think of Uma and his gang of robbers stripping those old rooms of the marvellous treasures there. The knocking went on and on, and they all stood and listened. Obviously the stone wall was very strong!

Then suddenly part of the wall gave way, and one of the big stones fell into the passage with a crash. The children heard it, though they were not near enough to see what had happened.

'The wall's giving way,' said Jack. 'They'll soon be through. Just stand here quietly and wait. Oola, stop that awful row. These are not gods who are coming, but men.'

'No, no – *Oola* say gods! *Tala* say gods!' moaned Oola. Tala had now climbed up the steps again, feeling his bruises with horror, and quite determined that, gods or no gods, he was not going to fall down those steps again. But as soon as he heard the knocking he almost repeated his performance, and only just clutched the rope in time. Fortunately the grappling hook held and he pulled himself to safety.

Another crash. That would be the stone next to the first one. Now it would be easy for the men to prise out two more and then creep in through the hole.

Crash! Thud! Then came shouts, echoing down the passage. Tala listened in astonishment. Why – these gods were speaking in his own language! He began seriously to doubt whether they *could* be gods! Oola listened too and stood up. Who were these gods who talked as men – who spoke the same words as he and Tala?

A light shone far away up the passage. 'One of the men is through,' said Philip. 'Ah – there's another light. Two men are through. Here they come!'

Two men, carrying torches, came down the passage cautiously, flashing the light here and there to see what kind of place they were in. They came suddenly upon the silent group of children, with Tala behind, and stared as if they could not believe their eyes. Philip stepped forward, about to speak.

But, in absolute panic, the men fled at top speed back to the broken wall, shouting in terror.

'Men frightened,' said Oola, in great satisfaction. 'Men go.'

'Come on – let's go to the wall and get through it ourselves,' said Philip. 'I'm longing for some good clean air
and the sun on my shoulders. I daresay it's a long, long
way up to the sun, but however long the climb it will be
worth it!'

They all moved up the passage, and came to the stone
wall. Tala shone his big torch on it, and they saw that four
great stones had been prised out and had fallen into the
passage. 'Come on,' said Philip. 'You go first, Jack, and
we'll follow.'

But at that moment a man looked through the hole,
and shone a torch right on them. He whistled.

'So the men were right. There *is* someone here – and
surely – surely it's Bill's little lot! Well, I'm blessed – is this
a dream? How did *you* get here?'

'Never mind that,' said Philip coldly. 'We have plenty
of questions to ask *you*, Mr Uma! Where are Bill and my
mother? Are they safe?'

Mr Uma didn't answer. He ran his torch quickly over
the little group to see how many there were. 'Was it you
who took my motor-boat?' he asked abruptly. 'Where is
it?'

'Never mind that,' repeated Philip. 'Tell me about my
mother and Bill. You're going to get into trouble about all
this, Mr Uma. We know all about your plans – you're
nothing but a robber!'

'You hold your tongue!' shouted Mr Uma, suddenly

losing his temper. 'How did you get here? There's no way in except this.'

'Oh yes there is,' said Philip. 'But it isn't one you are ever likely to find! Now, let us out of this hole, and tell us where to find Bill.'

Mr Uma then addressed Tala in his own language, and by his angry tone and fierce expression he was threatening Tala with all sorts of things. Tala listened stolidly to the questions and threats thrown at him.

'Tala not know, Tala not know,' he kept answering, in English, which really infuriated Mr Uma.

'What's he saying, Tala?' asked Philip.

'He say, how come we here? He say he catch us all, not let us go. He say many bad things. He bad man.' Tala suddenly spat at Mr Uma, who immediately flung his torch at him, hitting him on the cheek. Tala laughed, bent down, picked up the torch and put it into his waist-cloth. Then he stood gazing impassively at the angry Mr Uma.

Mr Uma shook his fist and then disappeared. They heard him shouting for his men.

'He send men to tie us up,' said Tala, listening. 'Mr Uma bad man, very bad man.'

'Will he really have us tied up?' asked Dinah fearfully.

'I shouldn't be surprised,' said Jack. 'He needs us out of the way while he steals what he wants from those treasure-chambers. Then, when he has taken all the best and most valuable things, he'll be off, and we'll be set free – I hope!'

'Beast!' said Dinah fiercely. 'I suppose he's got Mother and Bill tied up somewhere too.'

'Yes. Probably in his house at Chaldo,' said Philip. 'What are we to do? We can't fight a whole lot of men!'

'Let's climb through that hole in the cavern wall, and get back to the boat,' said Jack suddenly.

'Quite a good idea,' said Philip. 'Except that it leaves Uma free to rifle all through those store-rooms, and take what he pleases – and I've been hoping somehow we might be able to stop him.'

'We're too late,' said Lucy-Ann. 'Here come the men!'

She was right. A man came through the hole in the wall, and then another and another. It was too late now to run, for the men would follow them and see where they went. So the children stood their ground. Kiki, who had been silent for some time, was very excited when she saw the men squeezing through the hole. She jigged up and down on Jack's shoulder and gave a loud screech, which startled the men considerably.

There were now six men through the wall, and they came menacingly towards the children.

'Keep off,' said Philip commandingly. 'Don't lay hands on us, or you will get into serious trouble with the police!'

'Police!' screamed Kiki at once. 'Police! Fetch the police! PHEEEEEEEEEE! PHEEEEEEEEEEE!'

The men stopped abruptly, startled almost out of their

wits. The shrill whistle that Kiki gave echoed round and round the passage in a very terrifying manner. 'PHEEEEEEEE, PHEEEEEEEE, PHEEEEEEEE.' It went on and on – and then, to crown everything, Kiki added her noise of a motor-car back-firing. 'Pop! Crack! Crack!' These joined the whistling echoes, and alarmed the men so much that they turned and ran for the wall, adding their own screams to the crazy chorus of echoes!

The children laughed as they watched the men scramble through the wall in a panic.

'Thanks, Kiki,' said Jack, stroking the parrot's feathers. 'For once I shall not say, "Be quiet!" You came in at just the right moment!'

27

What now?

Tala laughed heartily as he saw the men scrambling to get away from the mysterious noises. His enormous guffaws filled the passage too. Oola danced about and clapped his hands in glee. Both appeared to think that now that they had put the men to flight all their troubles were over.

But the children knew better. They turned gravely to one another. 'Should we try to get through the hole ourselves, now there's a chance?' said Philip.

'I don't know. We are comparatively safe here, now that the men have been so frightened,' said Jack. 'What do you think, Tala? Will those men come back?'

'Men frighted, very frighted,' said Tala, showing all his white teeth. 'Men not come back. Never come back. We go then?'

'No. Wait a bit,' said Jack. 'We don't want to walk out of the frying-pan into the fire. The men will go to Uma, and tell him what happened – and he'll perhaps lie in wait for us, hoping to catch us as we climb through the wall.'

Tala nodded. 'That good talk. We wait. Uma much bad man.'

They sat down and waited. Nothing happened for a while, and then a man came to the hole in the wall. He wore a turban and white robes.

'I would speak with you,' he called, in a voice that was not quite English. Philip thought he might be a messenger of Uma's, and waited to see what he would say.

'I would come through the wall. I would speak with you,' repeated the man.

'Come through then,' said Philip, wondering who the man was.

The man squeezed through the hole and came over to the children. He had a very polite manner, and bowed gravely to them all.

'May I sit with you?'

'You may,' said Philip, on his guard. 'Why do you come?'

'I come to tell you that my friend, Mr Raya Uma, is sad that he has frightened you,' said the man. 'He was – how do you say it? – *startled* – at your being here. He said things that he is sorry for.'

Nobody said a word. Jack and Philip were all ears. What was Mr Uma's little game now?

'His men have been to him to say that they will not work for him any more,' went on the man, in his soft voice. 'They are too afraid. That is bad news for him. He must get others. So he has sent me to say that you may go unmolested. He will see that you are set on the right road, and he will lend you his biggest car, so that you may go back to Chaldo in safety.'

'Why Chaldo?' asked Philip at once.

'Because it is there that he has Mr Bill and his wife,' said the soft-spoken man. 'You will join them and can then do what you will. Is this agreeable to you?'

'Who are *you*?' asked Jack bluntly.

'I am his friend,' said the man. 'But I am not so hasty as he. I said he was wrong to frighten you, you are but children. He listens to me, as you see. Now – will you accept his generous offer? He is sincerely sorry for his foolishness.'

'Go and tell him we will think it over,' said Jack. 'We need to talk about it. We do not trust Mr Uma, your friend.'

'That is sad,' said the man, and he stood up. 'I go to wait outside the wall, and you will come to tell me when you have talked together. We are agreed?'

The man suddenly saw the golden bowl beside Tala, and stared at it in surprise.

'Where did you get that?' he asked. 'May I see it?' He bent down to pick it up, but Tala snatched it away, standing up with it held high in his hands. Uma's friend reached up for it, his white sleeves falling back over his bare arms. But Tala would not release his hold on the bowl. He said something rude in his own language, and the man looked as if he were about to strike him. But he recovered himself, bowed and walked off to the hole in the wall. He squeezed through it and stood waiting on the other side.

'Well – what about it?' said Philip.

Jack shook his head vehemently. 'No, no, no! Didn't you notice something when he reached up to get the bowl from Tala? He's no friend of Mr Uma's!'

'Who is he then?' said everyone, astonished.

'He's Mr Uma *himself*!' said Jack. 'Didn't you see his right fore-arm when he reached up for that bowl? His sleeve fell back – and there, on his arm, was the white scar of an old wound – just like a curving snake!'

There was a dead silence. Then Philip whistled. 'My word!' he said. 'The daring of it – coming to us like that – the cunning! It never once occurred to me that it was Mr Uma himself – dressed like the ordinary people – speaking the same kind of broken English. My, he's a cunning fellow! No wonder all those photos of him looked as if they were of different men!'

'Well!' said Dinah, astounded. 'Fancy having the *nerve* to come and talk to us like that! Trying to persuade us to walk right into a clever little trap. Good thing you saw that snake-like scar, Jack!'

'Good thing Bill *told* us about it!' said Jack. 'Well – what do we do now? Go and tell him it's no go, we know who he is?'

'Yes,' said Philip, getting up. 'Come on, we'll tell him now, Jack. You others stay here.'

The boys walked up the passage to the wall. Mr Uma, his hands folded inside his robes, waited impassively, looking for all the world like a distinguished man.

'Mr Uma,' said Philip boldly, 'we say no to your little trap.'

'What do you mean?' said the man. 'I am not Mr Uma! I am his friend. Do not be insolent, boy.'

'You *are* Mr Uma,' said Philip. 'We saw the snake-like scar on your right arm – your mark, Mr Uma, and a good one too – for your ways are surely as cunning as a snake's!'

Mr Uma cast away his soft voice and polite manners. He screamed at them, both his fists in the air.

'You bring it upon yourselves! I will teach you a lesson! You think you will walk out of here and up to the sun. You will not! You will not! I will block up this hole and you shall not come this way!'

'We'll go out the way we came then,' said Jack boldly. 'This is not the only way in.'

'Ah, you cannot go out the way you came in!' said Mr Uma. 'If you could, you would have left by now. I am not so foolish as you think. You need a lesson, and you shall have it!'

He called loudly, leaning away from the stone. 'Come here, men. Come! I have work for you to do!'

The children and Tala and Oola were now all beside the wall, listening. No men came in answer to Mr Uma's call. He shouted again in a language the children could not follow, and this time two men came, very reluctantly.

'Bring bricks! Block up this hole!' commanded Uma. The men stared at him sullenly, looking fearfully in through the hole, remembering what their comrades had said when they had come back from the passage beyond.

Uma began to talk very fast to them, and the men listened with sudden interest.

'What's he saying, Tala?' asked Jack.

'He promise gold,' said Tala. 'He say they rich men if they obey. Much, much gold.'

The men looked at one another and nodded. They went off and came back with a pile of bricks. A third man brought mortar, and the blocking up of the hole began.

The little company inside were in despair. They knew that they could go back to the boat and find plenty of food, and could get fresh air outside the cavern – but for how long was Uma going to imprison them? They would *have* to give in sooner or later. They watched the gradual filling-in of the hole – and then Philip suddenly had an idea!

He put his hand inside his shirt and gently eased out the bargua snake he still cherished. He slide the bright green creature on to the edge of the small hole still left in the wall, and held it there.

'Mr Uma!' he called. 'Mr Uma – are you there? Here is something for you!'

Uma came at once to the wall, and put his face near to

the hole, shining his torch into it. He saw the writhing bargua snake at once. He gave a scream of real panic as the snake came gliding out. The three men outside saw it too, dropped their tools and fled, shouting in terror.

'Bargua! Bargua!'

Nobody could see what happened next, for the other side of the hole was now in complete darkness. The children could hear nothing, after the cries had died away in the distance.

'Tala break wall,' said Tala suddenly. He took the little trowel he still had hanging round his neck and attacked the wall vigorously, Oola helping him with his bare hands. The mortar was still soft and it was not very difficult to force out the roughly-set bricks and make the hole as big as it was before.

'Good, Tala – good, Oola!' said Philip. 'Now, out we all get as quickly as possible, while the bargua is still scaring everyone. Ready?'

They squeezed out one by one and found themselves in a very narrow passage, evidently quite newly excavated. They went along it and came to what looked like a shaft going straight up. Rough steps were cut in the side and a rope hung down as a handhold.

'Well – up we go!' said Philip, shining his torch upwards. 'Good luck, everybody – this is our only chance of escape!'

28

Uma is in trouble

It was a long and difficult way up the deep shaft. Philip reached the top first, feeling quite worn out, for the footholds were none too good, and it was tiring work climbing, climbing, climbing, with only a thin rope to pull on.

He found himself still in darkness at the top, in a small narrow tunnel that sloped upwards. He stood at the top of the shaft to help Lucy-Ann out and then went to see where the passage led. It led to another shaft, but a much shorter one, for Philip could see daylight at the top. His heart leapt. Daylight again! What a wonderful thing!

Soon all the others had arrived safely up the shaft, though Tala was complaining bitterly. 'Tala slip,' he said. 'Tala hold rope, Tala burn hand, see!'

Poor Tala! He had slipped, and had slid down the rope so fast that he had scorched his hands on it. Philip handed him his handkerchief.

'Here you are. Bind it round,' he said. 'There is no

time to make a fuss. I wish I could see my bargua snake somewhere, but I can't.'

'You surely didn't expect it to climb the shaft, Philip!' said Dinah.

'Snakes can wriggle anywhere,' said Philip. 'Come on! There's another shaft to climb – then daylight!'

Everyone was delighted to hear that. They were soon climbing the next shaft, which was very much easier because it had a rope ladder hanging down the side. They were soon at the top.

'It's heaven to stand in the daylight again!' said Lucy-Ann, blinking at the brightness around. 'And doesn't this sun feel good, Dinah! Oh, Philip – you're surely not looking for the bargua up *here*. It *couldn't* climb two shafts, poor thing!'

Dinah was secretly very glad indeed that the spotted bargua had gone, but she didn't dare to say so, for it had been the cause of their sudden freedom. She stood looking round eagerly, delighting in the sunshine.

They were in a most desolate spot. 'Like a builder's yard in the middle of a dusty, sandy desert!' she said, and they all agreed.

'Where is everyone?' wondered Jack. 'Oh – there are the men over there. What are they doing – bending down over something.'

The men heard the voices and looked round. Then one of them came running at top speed, leaping over the mounds of dug-up earth. He signalled urgently to Philip and Jack, calling out something in his own language.

'What does he say?' asked Philip, turning to Oola and Tala, puzzled at the man's urgency.

Oola laughed triumphantly. 'He say bargua snake bite his master. He say master very frighted, will die, because bargua poison-snake. He say Mr Uma want to speak with you.'

The children looked at each other, and smiled small, secret smiles. They knew that the bargua snake had no poison, but it had bitten Mr Uma and now he thought he was certain to die – unless he was taken to a doctor at once and treated for snake-bite!

'*Could* your bargua bite?' asked Dinah, in a low voice. 'Even though it has no poison?'

Philip nodded. 'Oh yes – but its bite is now harmless. Well – this is rather funny. Let's go and talk to Mr Uma. He's evidently feeling very sorry for himself.'

They went over to where he was lying on the ground, so frightened that his brown face was almost white. He was holding his right arm and groaning.

'That snake – it bit me,' he said to Philip. 'You'll have caused my death unless you help to take me to Cine-Town at once. There are good doctors there – they may save me.'

'Your man Jallie told us that you had taken Bill and my mother to Wooti,' said Philip sternly. 'Answer me. Is that so? Are they there?'

'Yes. And the motor-launch too,' said Mr Uma feebly. 'We will go there at once. Mr Bill can take me in his launch to Cine-Town, away up the river – he shall find me a doctor. Help me, boy. I may not have long to live. Have mercy – it was *your* snake that bit me!'

Philip turned away, scorning this man who now cried for mercy and for help, although a short while back he had given orders to his men to brick them into the underground passage. He spoke to Tala.

'Please arrange this, Tala. There is a lorry over there, and a van. Tell the men to put Mr Uma into the van, and we will come in the lorry. Mr Uma will know the way. You drive the lorry, Tala, then if there is any trickery you can put your foot down hard and race us to safety.'

But there was no trickery this time. Mr Uma was in such a panic over the snake-bite that all he wanted to do was to get to Wooti and beg Bill to take him to Cine-Town as soon as possible.

They set off, the van leading the way and Tala following after in the lorry. Both were exceedingly well-sprung, strong vehicles, and this was just as well, for there was no real road to speak of. The lorry and van jerked and jolted over hills and mounds, and poor Mr Uma, lying in the van, cried out in misery as he rolled from side to side. He was not really ill, but he was so certain that his whole body was being poisoned by the snake-bite that he was sure he had aches and pains all over!

It was a long way to Wooti, but they got there at last.

Mr Uma gave his driver a few directions when they arrived, and both lorry and van stopped outside a shack set by itself beside a desolate cart-track.

The driver got down and took some keys from Mr Uma. He unlocked the door of the shack and out came Bill at once, looking more furious than the children had ever seen him look before.

'Now then!' shouted Bill. 'Where's that fellow Uma?'

The van-driver gesticulated and said a good deal. Evidently he was telling Bill about the snake-bite. Bill, however, was not at all sympathetic. Jack and Philip judged it time to say a few words themselves and they leapt out and ran over to Bill.

He stared at them as if he were dreaming. 'Jack! Philip! What on earth – good heavens, what *is* all this? Explain quickly, Philip.'

Philip explained a little, enough to make Bill understand what was happening at the moment.

'Uma's back in the van,' he said. 'He thinks he's been bitten by a poisonous snake – but he hasn't really, it was only my own bargua – and you know how harmless *that* was! He's so anxious to get to a doctor at Cine-Town up the river that he agreed to take us here and free *you*, so that you could take him in your launch to find a doctor. That's briefly what's happening now, Bill.'

'Well, I'm blessed,' said Bill again. 'So our friend Uma thinks he's been fatally bitten, does he? Then perhaps he would like to confess a few things and clear his conscience! Right – find out where the launch is, boys, tell Uma I'm coming, and I'll just go and fetch my wife.'

Bill ran off to the shack, and Philip, anxious to see his mother, went with him. Jack went to tell Uma that Bill was coming, and to ask where the launch was.

Uma was still very pale. He groaned. 'Good boy,' he said. 'Ah, this is a punishment for all my sins. I have been a wicked man, boy.'

'It sounds like it,' agreed Jack hard-heartedly. 'Bill wants to know where the launch is.'

'By the riverside,' groaned Mr Uma. 'The poison's working in my veins, I know it is! We shall have to hurry!'

Bill came out with his wife, who certainly looked none the worse for being locked up in the shack for a few days. She seemed quite cheerful, and had been told a little of the children's adventures by Philip. She and Bill had had no idea, of course, that the children had been through so much excitement.

They drove off to the river. Bill went in the van with Uma, who poured out such a lot of confessions that Bill was almost embarrassed. The things that Mr Uma had done in his life! His sins had certainly been very many.

The launch was by the river as Uma had said. By the time they reached it Mrs Cunningham had heard more of the children's news from everyone in the lorry, and had been greeted joyfully by Kiki, who insisted on shaking hands with her at least a dozen times.

'Pleasedtomeetyou,' said Kiki, running all the words together. 'Pleasedtomeetyou, good morning, goodbye!'

'Oh, Kiki – it's so nice to see you all again,' said Mrs Cunningham. 'We imagined that Tala would look after you, and that he would raise the alarm and bring help to us as soon as possible. I never realized you had been through a bad time like this! Poor Mr Uma – he must be in a terrible panic over this snake-bite.'

'Don't say "*poor* Mr Uma", Mother!' said Dinah. 'He's wicked. You wait till you hear *all* our story. It's hair-raising, really it is!'

The lorry and the van were left at Wooti, and the launch took everyone to Cine-Town, with Mr Uma tossing and groaning all the time. It seemed remarkable that he could simulate all the symptoms of snake-bite like this, and Bill half wondered if Philip's bargua had been as harmless as they had imagined!

He frowned as he thought of all the things that the scared Mr Uma had blurted out to him – and this latest plan to rob the old, forgotten temple of its priceless treasures for the sake of mere greed sickened Bill. Mr Uma was *not*, of course, being taken to see a doctor – no, he was being taken to see some very high-up police!

It was a really terrible shock to Mr Uma to be handed over to the police at Cine-Town, when they arrived there. Bill had ordered two cars as soon as the launch had reached Cine-Town, and he and his wife and Uma had gone in the first one, and the other six, with Kiki, in the second – and they had all driven to police headquarters. Mr Uma could hardly believe his eyes when he was half led, half carried into a bare police-station, instead of into the pleasant private room of a hospital that he had expected.

'What's this?' he cried. 'Is this a kind trick to play on a man dying of snake-bite – a poisonous snake-bite?'

'You're quite all right, Uma,' said Bill with a laugh. 'It *wasn't* a poisonous bite – the snake had unfortunately had its poison-ducts cut, and was no longer poisonous. So cheer up – you're not going to die – but you've got a tremendous lot of things to explain to the police, haven't you?'

29

End of the adventure

It wasn't only Uma who had to explain a great many things – it was the children too, who had so much to tell Bill and his wife that they felt it would take a week to finish their tale!

After Uma had been taken charge of by some much-amused police officers, who had heard the whole story from Bill and the others, they had been allowed to depart for the launch.

'The police seem to find it very funny that Uma is so disappointed not to have had a poisonous bite after all,' said Bill, as they left. 'Of course – it *is* bad luck when one's sins find one out – but they always have a nasty little habit of doing that. Crime simply does NOT pay!'

'Well, Uma's learnt that now – or do you think he hasn't?' asked Philip. 'Will he start his bad ways all over again, now he knows he *hasn't* been bitten by a poisonous bargua, Bill?'

'I fear he will have to disappear from public life for

quite a time!' said Bill. 'Long enough to get over any snake-bite, real or imaginary. I must say that snake of yours repaid you well for your kindness to him, Philip.'

'Yes. But I wish I could have got him back,' said Philip. 'I liked him.'

'Don't say that in front of Oola or he'll produce a few more barguas,' said Dinah, in a panic.

It was wonderful to laze on the launch again, and talk and talk. Bill was amazed at the children's adventures.

'There were we, cooped up in a silly shack with barred windows and a locked door and nothing whatever happening – and you four having the time of your lives,' he said. 'Rushing down gorges, almost shooting over cataracts, crawling through holes, exploring age-old treasures . . .'

'It was pretty tough at times,' said Jack. 'The girls were marvellous. And so were Tala and Oola!'

This was such an unusual compliment from Jack that both the girls stared in surprise.

'Kiki did *her* bit too,' said Jack. Bill laughed.

'She certainly did, from all you've told me!' he said. 'She seems to react marvellously to the word "police".'

'Police!' called Kiki at once. 'Fetch the police! PHEEEEEEEEEEEEEE!'

Some people stopped beside the launch at once, eyes round with fright.

'It's all right,' called Jack. 'It's only the parrot. Don't do

219

that too often, Kiki, or one of these fine days you'll find a policeman will come along and lock you up!'

'PHEEEEEEEEEEE!' began Kiki again, and got a tap on the beak.

'Bad boy!' she grumbled at Jack. 'Bad boy! Fetch your nose, blow the doctor!'

'It's nice to hear her again,' said Mrs Cunningham. 'Bill and I could have done with a bit of Kiki's fun those long dull days in that shack.'

'I suppose you know, you youngsters, that you have made the find of the century?' said Bill, after a while. 'I know that Uma was also on the mark, but he's a bit discredited at the moment – finding a place like that wonderful old temple merely to rob it is rather different from discovering it by accident as you did, and doing your best to keep off those who wanted to despoil it.'

'What do you think of the things we brought back, Bill?' asked Dinah eagerly. 'That gold bowl – it *is* gold, isn't it? – and the cup – and the little statue – and the dagger. Don't you think they are marvellous? I wish we could keep them, but I know we can't.'

'No, you can't. They belong to the whole world,' said Bill, 'not only to our own generation, but to all those who follow us. They are wonderful relics of the history of man – and I am prouder than I can say that you have had a hand in bringing them to light.'

'What will happen about the temple, Bill?' asked Jack. 'And what is going to happen to the things we brought back? – we had to leave them at the police station, you know.'

'Yes – well, they are being shown to some of the finest experts in the world,' said Bill. 'The police say that when the news gets round that this long-lost temple has been found, there will be many famous archaeologists flying here, anxious to see that any excavating is now done properly.'

'Shall we meet them?' asked Philip eagerly.

'No. You'll be at school,' said Bill hard-heartedly.

'*School!* Oh, Bill, you're *mean!*' said Dinah, who had imagined herself having a wonderful time talking learnedly to famous men. 'Aren't we going to stay on and see it all being dug out?'

'Good gracious, no!' said Mrs Cunningham. 'It may take five or six years – even more – to excavate that wonderful temple. It's not done in the haphazard way that Mr Uma did it, you know. Why, practically every piece of earth will be sifted!'

'Oh! How disappointing that we can't stay for the excitement!' sighed Lucy-Ann.

'My dear Lucy-Ann – haven't you had *enough* excitement already?' asked Bill, astonished. 'I should have thought that you four had had enough adventures to last the ordinary person for the rest of his life!'

'Well – perhaps we're not ordinary persons?' suggested Philip, with a twinkle in his eye.

'*You're* not an ordinary person, Philip!' said Dinah. 'I

wish you were! No *ordinary* person would take a snake about with him. I expect you'll adopt a camel next!'

'Well, that reminds me – Bill, I *did* see a baby camel today that didn't look too happy,' said Philip hopefully. 'I thought that if any prizes were going for brilliance in finding a long-forgotten temple, perhaps mine might be something like a baby camel.'

'Certainly not,' said Mrs Cunningham, sitting up straight. 'You can't be serious, Philip! What – take one *home*, do you mean!'

'Well, this was a very *little* one,' said Philip earnestly. 'Wasn't it, Lucy-Ann? Not more than two days old. It was absol—'

'Philip – do you or do you *not* know that camels grow very big – and that they do *not* like a cold climate like ours?' said his mother. 'And that I would *not* dream of having a camel sitting in the middle of my rose-beds, and . . .'

'All right, Mother, all right,' said Philip hurriedly. 'It was only just an *idea* of mine – and you both seemed so pleased with us that – well . . .'

'That you thought you'd make hay while the sun shone and cash in on a camel?' said Bill with a grin. 'No go, Philip, old son. Try something else.'

'I hope we're not going back to school *immediately*,' said Jack. 'I did rather want to show you that waterfall hurling itself over the edge of the gorge, Aunt Allie. Can't we go and explore a bit down in the old temple –

wouldn't we be allowed to, seeing that we found it? Then you could creep through that hole in the cavern wall and crawl out on to the ledge and go and stand on the platform, and see what Oola calls the "waterfalling" – it's unbelievable!'

'Oola find waterfalling, Oola show kind Missus?' said Oola's voice, and his small black head appeared round a corner.

'Oh! So there you are!' said Philip. 'Come here, Oola. Sit with us and tell how you went out all by yourself to find the waterfalling.'

Oola was very proud to tell his story. He would not sit down to tell it, but stood there, a small, lithe figure, still with the marks of bruises and weals on his back, his eyes sparkling as he told his tale.

Mrs Cunningham drew him to her when he had finished. 'You're a good little boy and a brave one, Oola,' she said. 'We shall never forget you.'

'My boss remember Oola too?' asked Oola, looking at Philip with love in his eyes.

'Always,' said Philip. 'And when we come back here, sometime in the future, to see the temple when it is all dug out, and its treasures on show, you must be here to guide us round, Oola. Promise?'

'Oola promise. Oola keep clean, Oola go to school, Oola do all things like boss say,' said the small boy valiantly. He gave an unexpected salute and disappeared, his eyes shining with proud tears.

There was a little pause after he had gone. 'I like him very much indeed,' said Lucy-Ann emphatically. 'Don't you, Jack?'

Everyone nodded vigorously. Yes – Oola had been as astonishing a find as any of the treasures in the temple. Would they ever see him again? Yes, of course!

'Well, we've talked so much that I really feel my tongue is wearing out,' said Mrs Cunningham. 'But I must tell you one thing to relieve your minds. We are not going to *fly* back home – we are going by sea, and we shan't be home for a week or more.'

'Oh – super!' cried Dinah, and the others agreed in delight. Another whole week – what luck!

'Do you think we shall have had enough convalescence by then?' asked Lucy-Ann. 'Shall we be *fit* to go back to school?'

'Good gracious – you're all as fit as fiddles!' cried Mrs Cunningham.

'Fiddles! Fiddle-de-dee!' shouted Kiki. 'Diddly-fiddly, cat and spoon!'

'You're getting a bit mixed up, old thing,' said Jack. 'Sign of old age! Now, don't peck my ear *off*, please!'

They all sat silent for a while, and listened to the river flowing past, lapping gently against the boat.

'The River of Adventure,' said Lucy-Ann. 'We couldn't have given it a better name. We ran into adventure all the way along its banks.'

'And *what* adventures!' said Jack. 'Oh, *don't* keep nib-bling my ear, Kiki, *pleeeeeeeeeeese!*'

'Pleeeeeece! Fetch the pleeeeeece!' shouted Kiki, and whistled. 'PHEEEEEEEEEEEEEEE!'

Goodbye, Kiki. You *always* have the last word!

Read all the exciting adventures
in this bestselling series

The  of adventure

Something very sinister is happening on the mysterious Isle of Gloom and the children are determined to uncover the truth!

But Philip, Dinah, Lucy-Ann and Jack are not prepared for the dangerous adventure that awaits them in the abandoned copper mines and secret tunnels beneath the sea.

The  of adventure

Why is everyone so afraid of the castle on the hill, and what dark secrets lurk inside its walls?

When flashing lights are seen in a distant tower, Philip, Dinah, Lucy-Ann and Jack decide to investigate – and discover a very sinister plot concealed within its hidden rooms and gloomy underground passages.

The *Valley* of adventure

Who are the two strange pilots, and what is the secret treasure hidden in the lonely valley where the children land?

Nothing could be more exciting than a daring night flight on Bill's plane! But Philip, Dinah, Lucy-Ann and Jack soon find themselves flying straight into a truly amazing adventure.

The *Sea* of adventure

A mysterious trip to the desolate Northern Isles soon turns into a terrifying adventure when Bill is kidnapped!

Marooned far from the mainland on a deserted coast, Philip, Dinah, Lucy-Ann and Jack find themselves playing a dangerous game with an unknown enemy. Will they escape with Bill and their lives?

The *Mountain* of adventure

Surely a peaceful holiday in the Welsh mountains will keep the children out of trouble! But the mystery of a rumbling mountain soon has them thirsty for more adventure.

Philip, Dinah, Lucy-Ann and Jack are determined to explore the mountain and uncover its secret, but first they must escape from a pack of ravenous wolves and a mad genius who plans to rule the world!

The *Ship* of adventure

An amazing voyage around the beautiful Greek islands becomes an exciting quest to find the lost treasure of the Andra!

Philip, Dinah, Lucy-Ann and Jack are plunged into a search for hidden riches – with some ruthless villains hot on their trail! Will they find the treasure before it's too late?

The *Circus* of adventure

Why did Bill have to bring the babyish Gustavus with them on holiday? Jack knows he'll only be trouble . . .

But when Gustavus is kidnapped, along with Philip, Dinah and Lucy-Ann, Jack bravely sets out to rescue them, leading him to a faraway land and the discovery of a plot to kill the King!

The *River* of adventure

A river cruise through ancient desert lands becomes a mysterious adventure when Bill disappears!

While Philip, Dinah, Lucy-Ann and Jack are desperately searching for Bill, they become trapped beneath a forgotten temple where no one has set foot for 7,000 years. What dangers lurk within, and will they ever escape?

A selected list of titles available from Macmillan Children's Books

The prices shown below are correct at the time of going to press. However, Macmillan Publishers reserves the right to show new retail prices on covers, which may differ from those previously advertised.

Enid Blyton

The Island of Adventure	978-0-330-44629-7	£4.99
The Castle of Adventure	978-0-330-44630-3	£4.99
The Valley of Adventure	978-0-330-44835-2	£4.99
The Sea of Adventure	978-0-330-44836-9	£4.99
The Mountain of Adventure	978-0-330-44837-6	£4.99
The Ship of Adventure	978-0-330-44839-0	£4.99
The Circus of Adventure	978-0-330-44834-5	£4.99
The River of Adventure	978-0-330-44838-3	£4.99

All Pan Macmillan titles can be ordered from our website, www.panmacmillan.com, or from your local bookshop and are also available by post from:

Bookpost, PO Box 29, Douglas, Isle of Man IM99 1BQ

Credit cards accepted. For details:
Telephone: 01624 677237
Fax: 01624 670923
Email: bookshop@enterprise.net
www.bookpost.co.uk

Free postage and packing in the United Kingdom